EMERALD

and the
Elf King

BECKY BIGGS

ISBN: 978-1-949372-00-7 (Paperback)
ISBN: 978-1-949372-01-4 (eBook)

Any references to historical events, real people, or real places
are used fictitiously. Names, characters, and places are prod-
ucts of the author's imagination.

Front cover by Zoe Draws Things

www.beckybiggs.com

DEDICATION

For Matt, my husband, best friend and partner. Thank you for fighting the battles of creativity, toddler parenting and pregnancy with me as I worked on this book.

For my mom. Thanks for giving me the gifts I needed to make magic with my words.

For my little princess, Sophia and my little prince, Porter. May you always follow your dreams as you've inspired me to do.

CONTENTS

CHAPTER ONE   1
A Hero is Born

CHAPTER TWO   7
Meet Maple

CHAPTER THREE   15
Emerald to the Rescue

CHAPTER FOUR   22
A Mother's Despair

CHAPTER FIVE   28
Daydreams and Nightmares

CHAPTER SIX   34
A Royal Inspection

CHAPTER SEVEN   39
A Division in Eseland

CHAPTER EIGHT   46
Emerald's Fifteenth Birthday

CHAPTER NINE   66
A Proposal

CHAPTER TEN   70
The Journey Begins

CHAPTER ELEVEN   75
Trapped

CHAPTER TWELVE   83
Working in a Troll Gang

CHAPTER THIRTEEN   89
Tallyweed Tea

CHAPTER FOURTEEN   99
A Happy Reunion

CHAPTER FIFTEEN   119
The Gifts

CHAPTER SIXTEEN   125
Ortland

CHAPTER SEVENTEEN   132
The Marsh Spirits

CHAPTER EIGHTEEN   140
The Evil King

CHAPTER NINETEEN   151
Wedding Gowns and Gifts

CHAPTER TWENTY   162
A Royal Double Wedding

CHAPTER TWENTY-ONE   175
As the Dust Settles

CHAPTER TWENTY-TWO   184
Get Better Maple

CHAPTER TWENTY-THREE   189
Happily Ever After . . . Until the Next Adventure

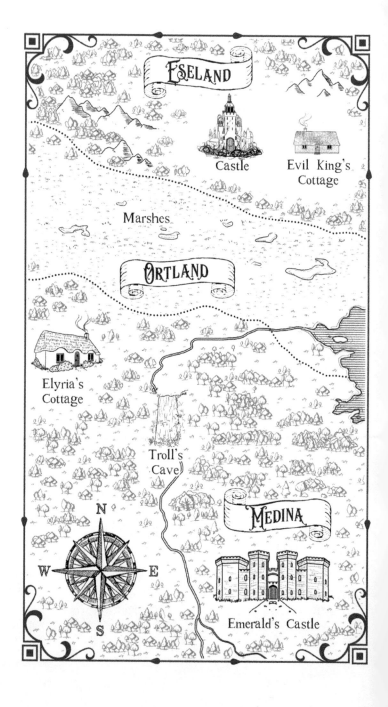

Chapter One

A Hero is Born

It was supposed to be a perfect day, but instead, the throne room was filled with panic. A wave of hushed, anxious chatter swept throughout the packed hall, echoing off the stone walls. Rumors are probably spreading like wild fire, King Argos thought ruefully, eyeing the crowds that filled the hall and spilled out into the courtyard. He sighed. The king preferred a peaceful life.

"Your Majesty?"

A voice heavily punctuated by rapid breathing brought King Argos out of his brooding. He stared down at the captain of his guard. The man he'd known since his youth was kneeling at the king's feet. The captain's chest rose and fell heavily beneath his shiny silver breastplate.

"Eseland is in chaos, you say?" King Argos shot a quick look at his wife. He could tell the wheels in her head were already turning. "Have there been any threats made to our kingdom?"

"Not as of yet, sire," the captain responded, trying to catch his breath. He'd ridden as hard and fast as he could from the border between the human kingdom of Medina and Ortland, the haunted marshland that separated the humans from the magical kingdom of Eseland to the north.

"However, we are starting to get large numbers of refugees from Eseland," the captain continued. "Sire, what should we do with them? We've never seen so many magical creatures before."

King Argos turned to his wife, not sure how to answer. Typically, the magical and non-magical worlds kept to themselves. Sure, the occasional centaur or pixie was reportedly spotted in the woods near Medina or close to some of the other southern kingdoms, but these reports were so infrequent that they merely felt like fairytales.

"We should ask my godmother what to do when she arrives," Queen Willow suggested gently. She was quick-witted and decisive where King Argos tended to second-guess himself. They made a good team, but there were no doubts who was truly in charge. "She probably knows what's going on in Eseland. In the meantime, we can't turn away those who need our help."

"Yes, you're right, my dear." King Argos nodded and turned to the captain. "Er, Ridalgo, please ensure that anyone who crosses the border from Eseland has food and shelter—but keep them together for now. We need to know what is happening up north before it trickles into our kingdom." He swallowed and thought, better if they keep their mess to themselves.

"You may go, Ridalgo," said King Argos. "Thank you, as always, my friend."

"Yes, Your Majesty." Ridalgo stood and bowed.

King Argos looked down at the gilded crib near his feet. His infant daughter, unaware of the tension in the room, was waving around her little fists and giggling. Oh, to be a baby again, he thought. Happiness is milk and your parent's arms. The queen cleared her throat and nudged him. Time to face the crowd. Sighing once more, he stood at his full height and addressed the audience.

"People of Medina," King Argos began loudly, "you are likely wondering what Captain Ridalgo was doing here. He brings news from Eseland. It seems King Spruce has turned on his people. We do not know the extent of the trouble, but many of the inhabitants have fled to us for refuge."

Gasps undulated throughout the room and anxious voices piped up. "Magical creatures? Here?" "Where are they going to stay?" "How long will they be here?" "My mother says imps are thieves and elves have no boundaries."

The queen raised her hand to quiet the chatter. "We are still getting the details. In the meantime, we must be good hosts to our guests."

"Is he coming for us next?" a female voice timidly asked.

"No," King Argos said, a little uncertainly. After a nod from Queen Willow, he continued in a more confident voice. "No, we have no reason to think he is a threat to us."

Though his words were positive, King Argos could still feel the tension in the room. Queen Willow clapped her hands.

"Now, who's ready for a party?" she asked brightly, flashing a brilliant smile. "It's time to name our little princess. Long have we waited for her."

The cheers that went up in the room seemed a bit half-hearted until the king scooped up his daughter and held her high for all to see. The baby looked around curiously but didn't cry. The cheer that arose from the crowd this time was truly heartfelt.

"Please meet your new princess," King Argos said, his proud voice audible above the applause as he showed off his pride and joy.

The baby was dressed in an ornate white gown that the queen had worn on her own naming day. She had a patch of bright red hair, like her father's, that was visible to the back of the room. Those closest to the throne could see she also had striking green eyes, just like her mother.

King Argos scanned the crowd, looking for any hint of fear or anxiety. All he could see was admiration for his tiny daughter. He felt himself letting out a sigh of relief as he heard the gentle cries of "oooh" and "ahhh" rippling through the large audience. Just peace and happiness. Nothing more was going to dampen their spirits today.

The princess's naming ceremony was the biggest celebration the kingdom had ever seen. The castle was packed from courtyard to throne room with guests excited to bestow gifts on the baby. A line of people stretched far across the drawbridge and into the streets of the village, waiting to meet the newest member of the royal family.

Queen Willow stepped up next to her husband and took her daughter from him. The tiny diamonds encrusted on her deep blue gown shimmered and cast speckles of light all around her with every move. She seemed like a fairy queen herself, the effect amplified by the bejeweled crown sitting atop her pile of perfectly coiffed golden-blonde hair. She was simply stunning—the epitome of a perfect queen. The king was also dressed in his finest suit of royal blue and was wearing his own ornate crown, but he knew he could never hold a candle to his wife—not that he really cared.

"We have named her Emerald Aurora Rose," said the queen, deep love radiating from every inch of her body as she looked at her daughter. "Not only because of her beautiful eyes, but because she is so precious to us."

The crowd responded with a unanimous murmur of approval. Just like her mother, Princess Emerald was perfect in every way.

The queen then laid her daughter back in the golden crib and the guests began processing up to lay gifts at the feet of the princess. Though it took quite some time, the princess stayed awake and watched the passing of each person with alert, curious eyes. As the last guests approached the crib, the queen turned to the king anxiously.

"She said she was going to be here," Queen Willow whispered as she looked around the nearly empty throne room. "Do you think she's caught up in whatev—"

She was cut off by the sound of a woman's voice from the rear of the room. The last of Emerald's admirers turned and parted to watch in awe as a sprightly old woman with pearl-colored curls, a glittering lavender gown, and light-blue cloak glided elegantly to the foot of the thrones. Though her appearance alone might not have been enough for a second glance, she emanated an otherworldly aura that caused anyone who encountered her to stare in wonderment.

"I'm not too late, am I?" the enchanting old woman asked, bowing deeply to the king and queen.

Queen Willow immediately descended the four stairs from the top of the throne dais to the bottom and hugged the woman.

"My dear godmother," she cried. "I was starting to worry you wouldn't come. You aren't too late at all! Please, meet our darling daughter, Emerald." The queen escorted her godmother to the crib where they both stared adoringly at the cooing baby.

"Would you do us the honor of being godmother to Emerald?" the queen implored of the old woman as they admired the child. Her godmother's violet eyes glistened as she smiled and nodded, happily accepting her role as godmother to the next generation.

"Thank you for the great honor, Your Majesties," she said. Then she looked at the queen. "I'll watch over her just as I've watched over you and over your mother before you." Turning to Emerald, she leaned over the crib and gently touched the baby's forehead.

"I see great things ahead for you, my little one," Elyria whispered to her new goddaughter, her eyes blooming with tenderness. "The going won't be easy, but you will have the bravery, strength, and cleverness to see you through." Emerald's new godmother gently kissed the baby and Emerald waved her tiny fists. The king, queen, and old woman smiled dotingly back at the baby.

Yes, Emerald was absolutely perfect.

Chapter Two

MEET MAPLE

After Emerald's godmother bestowed her blessing on the little baby, the remaining guests in the throne room were encouraged to head to the royal dining room or one of the great tents outside to continue their celebrations. The king and queen, however, held back and asked the old woman to stay with them.

"We received word today that Eseland is in chaos and that the inhabitants are flooding our border," King Argos began. "Elyria, do you know anything about this?"

The old woman sighed deeply. She untied and removed her blue cloak, placing it gently on a stool near the thrones.

"It's not the news I wanted to bring on such a special day." She turned back to the king and queen. "You'll remember King Spruce and Queen Ivy, of course?" The king and queen nodded. "They had a daughter—Raina—about five years ago."

"Oh yes," Queen Willow agreed. "We sent them a gift for the baby. We were so happy for them, though it was such a difficult time for us."

King Argos covered his wife's hand and Elyria nodded understandingly and said, "I know how much you both suffered with wanting a child."

"Yes," Queen Willow responded with a smile, her green eyes glistening. "And now we have been blessed with our beautiful Emerald."

7

"Indeed you have," Elyria said warmly. "King Spruce and Queen Ivy were just as happy about their little girl. Unfortunately, she was born without magic. They were devastated."

"That seems like a small price to pay for having a healthy child," Queen Willow muttered, looking at her own daughter.

"Perhaps"—Elyria cocked her eyebrow thoughtfully at the queen—"but it is different in Eseland. A child, especially a royal one, without magic is considered extremely unlucky. Many are even sent away to live in the human kingdoms, including Medina."

The king and queen looked at each other in surprise. Were there magical children living in their kingdom? How had they not known this?

"Ridalgo, captain of your guard, is one," Elyria said, as if reading their minds. The king shook his head in disbelief. He'd known Ridalgo since they were children.

"Not that you would really know," Elyria continued. "It's typically only elves or nymphs that are affected. They can easily pass as human, and the children are adopted at such a young age, they don't remember otherwise."

"I can't believe they don't appreciate all of their children, regardless of whether they are different or not." Queen Willow creased her lovely brow and huffed.

"Yes, it's unfortunate, but that's how things are done in Eseland. There are many who don't agree with the practice, but it's especially hard to hide when the child is royal. Which brings me to what's happening in Eseland." Elyria smoothed her hair back and gestured at the thrones. "We might want to sit, if it suits Your Majesties. My story is a long one and I have traveled far."

"How thoughtless of us," King Argos said immediately.

Red-faced, he offered his throne to Elyria. "Please forgive us for keeping you standing for so long."

Elyria waved her hand in dismissal of his apology but gratefully sat on the king's throne as he took a seat for himself on a footstool next to her. Emerald was now peacefully sleeping in her crib.

"Raina had no magic, but King Spruce and Queen Ivy were determined that no one should find out," Elyria said after they were all comfortably settled in. She looked pointedly at Queen Willow. "They didn't like the idea of sending their child away."

"They're the king and queen! Why didn't they just order everyone to accept non-magical children?" Queen Willow looked indignant.

"Sometimes tradition is hard to change, even for a king and queen." Elyria gave another meaningful look to the queen. Queen Willow and King Spruce looked at each other in confusion.

"They came to me and asked for my help, but I declined," Elyria continued, without harping on the subject of tradition any further. "I warned them that they should not try to force magic upon her. Those who do not have it can never learn to control it." Elyria rubbed her temples tiredly, suddenly looking much older. "Unfortunately, King Spruce and Queen Ivy didn't heed my advice. They decided to take matters into their own hands."

"What did they do?" King Argos asked eagerly, enthralled with the tale. As much as he hated real-life drama, the king loved a good story.

"There is a troll who lived in Ortland," responded Elyria. "He's a good sort, though rather…misguided. Harry is his name. He caused some mischief about thirty years ago with some magic fires and was forced out of Medina.

Misguided as he is, Harry is also very powerful—and a bit of a pushover. It didn't take much for King Argos to convince him to help Raina."

"Trolls have magical powers too?" King Argos marveled. He'd always been curious about his neighbors to the north. His wife wouldn't hear of them opening the borders, though.

"Yes." Elyria smiled knowingly. "Harry created a stone that would give Raina magic powers, but it came at a terrible cost. The stone needed to steal powers from others to give it magic. It also sucked a little bit of the soul of its master each time she used it."

"What a terrible thing to present to a child," Queen Willow exclaimed, shocked. A poorly timed cheer arose from the tents outside. The king chuckled awkwardly at the coincidence.

"Yes," Elyria agreed, ignoring the cheers and chuckling king. "But King Argos and Queen Ivy were desperate. Harry was worried about the damage his stone could cause. He convinced the king and queen to let him stay and tutor the princess in how to use it." Elyria sighed deeply before going on. "Magic can do wonderful things, but in the hands of the wrong person, it can also be very destructive."

"The princess was corrupted?" gasped Queen Willow. King Argos looked just as alarmed.

"No," Elyria responded, shaking her head. "It was her father."

"Her father?" Confused, King Argos shifted in his chair. In her crib, Emerald gurgled and stirred.

"Yes, the draw of the stone's power was too much for him," Elyria said sadly. "Before anyone in Eseland knew what was happening, creatures began losing their power. They were frightened and, of course, went to their king and queen for help. That help was refused—for obvious reasons. It didn't take long for anyone to figure out that something was wrong at the castle. At first, they blamed Harry. He would be a likely suspect, of course. They finally came to me for help but"—Elyria swallowed hard and her voice dropped nearly to a whisper—"I was almost too late."

"Do you need a bit of refreshment, godmother?" Queen Willow asked gently, looking worriedly at the old woman who was now ashen. The queen raised her hand to order something to eat and drink, but Elyria shook her head.

"No, my dear, I'm fine," she said. "I wish I could say the same for the royal family of Medina. You see, by the time I arrived at the castle last week, King Spruce had nearly lost his mind. I found him in the tower threatening Harry. Harry was just trying to get the king to see his madness. You can't argue with lunacy, though."

"What happened next?" The voice of King Argos startled Elyria who had gone quiet and was looking off in the distance, trapped in her memory. She shook her head as if to clear it and remember where she was.

"Well, I didn't quite know what was happening for a few minutes," Elyria said, starting her story again a bit shakily. "Truthfully, I thought Harry was the one abusing the stone. But when King Spruce tried to steal my magic, I realized what was really going on. I nearly passed out as my magic was draining, but Harry was brave. He fought the king. He won, but it cost Queen Ivy her life. The stone came loose in the struggle and struck her in the head. It killed her instantly."

"Oh no," gasped Queen Willow. "What about the princess? What happened to her?"

"She was…" Elyria's voice trailed off and she swallowed before continuing, pain deep in her purple eyes. "She was embracing her mother as Queen Ivy died. I can't imagine how she'll cope, poor child."

Elyria, King Argos, and Queen Willow simultaneously looked at the sleeping Princess Emerald, their hearts sinking for the other princess.

"King Spruce was beside himself with grief," Elyria finally said after a few moments of silence. "I banished him to Ortland with Raina. I couldn't bear to tear the child from her father. And Harry has been instructed to protect the stone with his life."

Elyria stood and stretched her weary joints. The recent events in Eseland had taken their toll on her. "The immediate danger is over, but there are still many creatures in Eseland who are frightened. I know Medina has kept its borders closed to magical creatures since your great-grandmother died, dear Willow, but I'm hoping you can feel compassion for those who are too scared to stay in Eseland. Shelter them. At least for a little while. As a favor to me."

"Yes, let them come," replied Queen Willow passionately. She stood and began pacing back and forth, as she always did when she was thinking hard. "What happened with my great-grandmother was years ago. It's about time we treated our neighbors as friends rather than enemies." She paused and turned to King Argos to gauge his reaction. "We will do our best to keep them safe until they are ready to return home."

"Absolutely," agreed the king as he stood and took Elyria's hand in his. "Think nothing of it. Our home is their home."

"Thank you. You are both so kind," Elyria squeezed the king's hand gratefully in response. "I sense this is only the beginning of the magical and non-magical worlds needing each other."

She turned to her new goddaughter, who was still sleeping, and murmured, "Bless the innocence of the child. Hers will be a different world than we've all known." Elyria looked thoughtfully at the baby for a moment before turning back to the king and queen. "I have one more favor to ask of you."

"Certainly, anything!" Queen Willow looked at the king who nodded in agreement.

Elyria turned toward the back of the room and beckoned at someone who was hidden behind the long green curtains that hung suspended from the large windows. A small wood imp in a maid's uniform stepped shyly from her hiding spot.

"This is Maple. She used to work in the castle in Eseland. I was hoping she could find a new home here. Perhaps she could be a companion to the princess."

The king and queen smiled at the shy creature, who was only as tall as the queen's knees, and nodded in affirmation.

"Of course," Queen Willow said before stretching out her hand to the wood imp. "Welcome home, Maple."

"Thank you, Your Majesty," Maple responded gladly. She had shoulder-length, curly purple hair and mischievous silver eyes. She appeared to be about eleven years old, but it was always hard to tell a wood imp's age. They were blessed with eternal youth. "Could I trouble you for some of that refreshment you offered earlier?"

Queen Willow laughed. "Yes, you must be famished from your journey. I'll order something for you immediately."

"Be careful with that one," Elyria warned as she looked at the imp fondly. "She'll empty your pantry if you let her."

Maple wrinkled her nose and stuck her tongue out at Elyria, causing the three adults to laugh. The imp shrugged and walked over to the cradle where Emerald was just stirring. The princess opened her eyes and gave a big smile to Maple. Maple grinned back and offered the baby one of her fingers, which Emerald grabbed with surprising strength.

"I think she likes me," Maple said happily. She started making faces at the princess, causing her to coo and wave her little arms in delight. King Spruce, Queen Willow, and Elyria watched the scene with glad hearts.

"Now, I hope you'll forgive my hasty departure," Elyria said, standing and tying her cloak back around her shoulders, "but I have some work to do back in Eseland. I really hoped to stay longer, but I'm afraid I'm needed in the north."

"We understand," the queen responded before adding, "Oh Godmother, thank you for being here."

"You're welcome," the old woman said, embracing the queen. "My dear, one last thing . . ."

"Yes," the queen responded, leaning back a bit to regard her godmother.

The old woman looked at the baby's crib with furrowed brows. "Remember, just because things are different, it doesn't make them bad."

Before the queen could ask for clarification, the old woman swept quickly out of the room. The king and queen looked anxiously at each other and then back down to their daughter. Whatever did she mean?

Chapter Three

EMERALD TO THE RESCUE

"Do you think this is chicory?" Emerald asked her friend Maple as she gently touched the light blue petals of the flower before her. They were at the edge of the woods that backed up to the stables behind the castle.

"Let me see the book," Maple responded, accepting a worn, leather-bound book from Emerald and handing the princess a half-eaten apple in return. The two friends found the book in the castle library. They were convinced that there might come a day when they needed to know which plants were edible as they went on a mission to save another kingdom from an invasion of giants.

"Well, it does have a hairy stem," Maple said, looking back and forth between the description in the book and the live plant. "And the flower looks like the drawing . . . but—"

She was interrupted by shouts deeper within the castle woods. Emerald and Maple looked at each other in alarm.

"Sounds like the baker's boy again," murmured Emerald.

"And I'll bet he's picking on someone."

Emerald and Maple crept closer to the noise, staying hidden behind a clump of bushes. Sure enough, the baker's boy was leading a small gang of children in tormenting a little elf boy. The elf was backed up against a tree. In addition to the baker's son, another young boy and two young girls surrounded the elf in a semi-circle, pulling their ears out in mockery of the poor creature and throwing clumps of mud at him.

"Why don't you just fly out of here? I'll bet those ears could take you anywhere!" said the baker's son, Throckton, in a mocking voice. He threw a clump of mud at the elf as if to encourage the creature to take flight.

Emerald and Maple looked at each other and nodded in agreement. They dropped the apple and book and dashed out from their observation point behind the group. They pushed their way through the children and stood protectively in front of the elf boy with their hands on their hips and a fierce look on their faces.

"Stop, in the name of the king!" Emerald demanded, her green eyes flashing and her fiery hair surrounding her head like the mane of a lion.

"Or what?" chortled Throckton. The tallest and broadest of the children, he wasn't afraid of anything. Or anyone.

"Or I'll tell my father that you are harassing the magical children," responded Emerald haughtily. She wished she had a sword. That would probably be more threatening.

"No, you won't," Throckton said, grinning. He scooped up more mud, rolled it into a ball, and began throwing it up and catching it. "Unless you want me to tell your daddy I saw you sword fighting with the stable boy."

"You wouldn't dare," Emerald sputtered, flushing a bright crimson that nearly matched the color of her hair.

"I would and you know it," he answered. "And then they'll lock you in your classroom and throw away the key." He added in a nasal falsetto, "Emerald, you need to behave more like a princess and less like a peasant child."

The three other kids in the gang laughed at his impression of the queen. Encouraged by their reaction, Throckton continued. "And then they'll throw your precious little stable boy in the dungeons. Buh-bye, horse boy!" he said, evilly.

Emerald's green eyes narrowed and she gave Maple a look

that said, "let's do this." With a shriek, the two of them attacked the gang of children. The elf boy took the opportunity to sneak away while the other children were embroiled in a fracas of flailing arms, flying mud, and kicking legs. Though she was tiny, Maple was fierce and she fought just as savagely as any of the other children.

"Stop! NOW!" A deep voice interrupted the fray. The cluster of children froze and they turned to find the stable boy. At sixteen years old, he towered over all of them and had a lean, muscular build that gave him an authoritative presence.

"Porter!" Emerald said happily. She had no brother of her own but loved the stable boy like he was one.

"Emerald." He nodded at her. "You better get back to the castle. I heard your mother is looking for you."

"Oh no! I'm late for my sewing lesson again," Emerald cried. "Come on, Maple! Maybe we can sneak in through the back."

The two friends darted off toward the kitchen in hopes of creeping up one of the castle's hidden passages. As they left, they heard Porter's gruff voice directed at the remaining children.

"As for the rest of you, you'll come with me and muck the stables," he instructed. There were audible groans from the children. "Now—if you know what's best for you."

The children obeyed. Porter was not one to be tested.

Just as Emerald and Maple darted out of the hidden doorway next to Emerald's fireplace, they came face-to-face with the queen. She looked as surprised to see them as the two friends were to see her, but the queen's face quickly darkened as she looked the girls up and down. Both were covered in mud and their new dresses had tears in them.

"Look at you two!" exclaimed Queen Willow, looking at her eight-year-old daughter in dismay. The little princess stood before her mother with her head bowed. Her green silk dress now boasted a torn sleeve and assorted splatters of mud. Her hair was a wild, flaming mess.

"What am I going to do with you?" Queen Willow cried in exasperation.

Emerald's eyes darted down furtively to Maple, who looked half-worried and half-defiant. Maple's matching dress didn't look much better.

The queen threw her hands up in the air. "Why can't you behave more like a princess? And, Maple, I expect you to set a good example for Emerald!"

"But, Mama, they were picking on the little elf boy," Emerald said defiantly. "I had to stop them."

"The baker's boy again?"

"Yes, he, the cook's son, and the seamstress's twins."

"They're a bad group, Your Majesty," Maple added for good measure.

The queen sighed. This wasn't the first time human children had picked on the magical ones. While some (adults included) had accepted the newcomers with open arms, others were highly suspicious of the refuges from Eseland and just wanted them to go back home, even after all these years.

"Why didn't you just find an adult?" she asked, rubbing her forehead with a slender and graceful hand.

"There was no time," insisted Emerald. "You and Daddy always say that it's the job of the king and queen to protect the kingdom and the citizens in it. That's what I was doing—as future queen!"

"Well, that is true," the queen said slowly. "But a queen does not fight. Her job is to deal with problems diplomatically. Something you would know if you took your lessons more seriously."

"I do, but Mama," Emerald started unhappily, "didn't you ever feel like you had to fight to save someone?"

"I did once," the queen said, her beautiful face relaxing into a more thoughtful expression. "When I was about your age, my sister was going to be spanked for tearing her dress while playing outside"—she gave Emerald a sharp glance—

"Something you're lucky I don't do to you." After a brief stare down between mother and daughter, the queen continued, "I didn't think my sister deserved a spanking, so I slapped my mother. I was dreadfully scared when I realized what I'd done. I was sure that was the end of me. Your grandmother turned to me and just said coolly, 'A queen must never act in violence. She must always be the steady, peaceful face of the kingdom.'"

"You smacked GRANDMOTHER?" Emerald gasped, shocked. Her grandmother was one of the most formidable people she'd ever met. Emerald couldn't imagine anyone, let alone her mother, slapping her.

"Yes," Queen Willow answered regretfully. "It was not the proudest moment of my life."

"Did she keep spanking Aunt Bella?" Emerald asked, enthralled.

"No," the queen responded, shaking her head. "She stopped. Maybe she realized that spanking was itself an act of violence. Whatever her reason, though, she never touched either of us in anger again. And that was the last time I ever responded to a situation physically."

"But, Mama," said Emerald, taking advantage of her mother's introspective mood, "what if you have no choice but to fight? Like, what if a dragon is attacking the kingdom or something?"

"Well, that's what you'll have a king for." The queen chuckled.

"Ugh! I'm not going to ever have a king. I can rule just fine by myself."

Queen Willow smiled. "I'm afraid, my dear, you don't have a say in the matter. It is your duty to one day marry and produce your own heirs to the throne. That is the greatest role of a queen."

"That's so boring! And unfair," grouched Emerald.

"Perhaps so, my child," Queen Willow said gently. "But is it fair for the farmer to work from sunrise to sunset and still sometimes lose his crop? We must live the life we are dealt as best we can."

She then clapped her hands and turned her attention to Maple. "Maple," she said. "I expect you to set a good example for Emerald. She needs your encouragement!"

"Yes, Your Majesty," the wood imp responded timidly, hanging her head. Sometimes it was very hard for a wood imp to behave, especially when Emerald needed her help fighting injustice in the world.

"Darling, I know it's not always easy to behave like a princess, especially when you are young," Queen Willow said, turning back to her daughter. "But it would mean so much to your father and me if you would put as much energy into your studies as you do into fighting. And if you could keep your dresses clean."

"Yes, Mother," Emerald answered dutifully. She really wanted to honor her mother's wishes. She just didn't always agree with her. It made her tummy twist and her insides feel rubbery to be so at odds with both her mother and herself.

"Now get cleaned up, you two. It's too late for that sewing lesson, but it is almost time for dinner," Queen Willow instructed before sweeping out the door.

After she left, Emerald turned to her friend and whispered, "When I'm queen, princesses will be allowed to fight if they need to. I won't care if my daughter gets muddy if it's for a good cause!"

"Yeah!" Maple whispered back, excitedly. "We can fight dragons and monsters and even if our dresses get dirty, it won't matter because we can just get new ones!"

Chapter Four

A Mother's Despair

"So, what did ye do this time?" Viola, Emerald's nursemaid, asked while scrubbing the dirt from under Emerald's fingernails. By this point, she was accustomed to Emerald and Maple returning to her covered in mud and in need of wardrobe repairs.

"It was the baker's son," piped up Maple from the adjoining tub. Her lavender hair hung in damp strands around her face, making her look somewhat like a wet puppy. "He and his gang were picking on the elf boy again. Emerald bravely fought them off." She added unabashedly, "I helped too."

"That wee rascal." Viola sighed. "He could use a good whipping. His father's no better. He was trying to rally a group at the pub earlier this week. Wants to get the magical folk out. Says they're why folks are getting so sick—" She stopped suddenly and glanced at Maple. "Oh, me and my big mouth. I shouldn't be telling stories." She helped Emerald out of the tub and wrapped her with a thick towel that had been warmed by the fire. "Now, what are we going to put ye two in? Do ye even have a dress without a tear?"

Viola hurried over to Emerald's wardrobe and away from the conversation. Emerald turned and helped Maple out of the tub, handing her a smaller but equally warm towel.

"It's getting worse," Emerald whispered to Maple.

"Are they going to send me back?" Maple whispered back, her eyes wide with fright. "I can't go back there. I just can't."

"No, I won't let them," Emerald said, hugging her tight. "I'll fight every person who wants to send you away if I have to."

The friends smiled at each other. Nothing could tear them apart.

"Now then, let's get ye dressed," Viola interrupted, returning to the girls with deep blue gowns covered in tiny yellow silk flowers. Once she had them appropriately attired and their hair bound up, she ushered them out the door to head to dinner.

As they passed the queen's chambers, Emerald and Maple heard raised voices coming from Queen Willow's room. Emerald's mother and godmother sounded almost like they were arguing. Looking around and finding the hallway empty, Emerald and Maple crept to the door to listen. It wasn't fully shut, so they could still see some of the room.

"I'm begging you to help her—help us," the queen pleaded as she wept in Elyria's arms. "She's such a fighter! I'm worried that she's never going to calm down and act like a queen. And then what prince will want her? Our kingdom will be doomed. Emerald will be doomed!"

"Hush, child," responded Elyria gently. "Everything will be just fine. I promise."

The queen sniffed and looked up at Elyria with red eyes and a tear-streaked face. "What if you used a little magic? Nothing much—perhaps just a happiness spell?" Queen Willow paused uncertainly. "Make her happy to be a normal princess?"

Out in the hallway, Emerald and Maple stared at each other, shocked. Emerald raised her hand as if to push the door open and interrupt the conversation, but Maple put her own hand on Emerald's arm and shook her head. Emerald nodded and stayed put as tears began to well up in her eyes.

"Emerald is the way she was meant to be," Elyria responded. "Remember, just because something is different, it doesn't make it bad."

The queen began pacing in and out of view.

"Doesn't make it bad?" the queen sputtered, her face as red as the cherry-colored gown she was wearing. "Are you serious? The different you warned us about was Emerald? You knew all along and you didn't see fit to better prepare us for her . . . her . . . differences?"

"My dear, please calm down and think rationally." Elyria approached the queen and put a hand on her arm. "Is having a princess who isn't afraid to stand up for others really such a bad thing?" She gave Queen Willow a meaningful look. "I recall another young princess who used to be quite energetic as well."

"Yes, and then I learned what my responsibilities were and how to act like the queen I was meant to be. Emerald is our only child. So much rides on her ability to reign." The queen's shoulders suddenly sagged and the energy seemed to drain from her. "Please, please help us—help Emerald!"

"I'm sorry. I really am, but there's nothing I can do." Elyria tried to take the queen's hands, but Queen Willow pushed her away.

"If you don't want to help Emerald—to be a godmother to her—then leave," Queen Willow spat bitterly. "I don't want to see your face around here again."

"Willow, darli—" the old woman started, but the queen suddenly snapped into full fury.

"Get. Out. NOW!" she demanded coldly, pointing at the door. Emerald and Maple gasped and threw themselves back at the wall. There was a moment of silence before the sound of Elyria's footsteps drew closer to the door. Emerald and Maple looked around desperately for a hiding spot, but there was no time to flee. The door opened and Emerald's godmother stepped out, the sound of the queen's sobs following behind her. Elyria saw Emerald and Maple right away but held a finger to her lips as she closed the door. She ushered the two friends a little farther up the hallway before speaking.

"Emerald, did y— How much did you hear?" Elyria asked, looking flustered and very unlike her usual composed self.

"I heard it all," Emerald responded, her shoulders slumping to match her fallen face. "I didn't realize I was such a disappointment to Mama and Daddy."

"I'm so sorry you had to witness that," Elyria said, embracing her goddaughter. "Your mother's wishes—they come from a good place. She doesn't understand you now, but she will." Elyria took the princess's face in her hands and looked deep into her goddaughter's green eyes. "Don't change. Whatever happens, stay true to yourself," she murmured. Then she turned and, reaching into a bag at her side, pulled out a thick, leather-bound book. "Read this when you feel like no one understands you."

"What is it?" Emerald asked, turning the book around in her hands. The cover was simple with nothing more than a rose embossed on it. Emerald flipped it open and inhaled the scent of old paper. It smelled wonderful.

"This is about your great-grandmother," Elyria responded. "I think you'll find a kindred spirit in her. Don't let anyone see you with it. It's forbidden to talk about Queen Ellyn. Now, I must go." Elyria pulled her blue cloak out of her bag and pulled it around her shoulders.

"No, you can't!" Emerald cried. "I'm sure Mama didn't mean it!"

Elyria looked at Emerald sadly as she fastened the cloak

around her neck. "I'm sure she didn't either. Still, I will honor her wishes. There are some things that need to be worked out between a mother and a daughter."

She bent and kissed Emerald on the head, whispering as she did so:

"A wish for you, my dear sweet child, With lovely looks and spirit wild, Your future is bright, you will see When the time is right, come to me."

Elyria then turned to Maple with a solemn look on her face. "You take good care of our Emerald."

"Yes, ma'am," Maple answered seriously, bowing to Elyria. Impish as she may be, Maple had honest respect for Elyria.

"Now go to your mother," Elyria said, turning back to Emerald. "She needs you. Sometimes you must fight a battle with compassion rather than physical strength."

Emerald nodded and gave her godmother one more hug. She and Maple watched Elyria wave her wand and vanish.

"I should face her alone," she said to Maple. The imp nodded. Emerald turned and walked back to her mother's room as Maple scurried away to give the princess some privacy.

When Emerald opened the door, she saw the queen still crying on her bed. She felt a pit in her stomach. Softly she tiptoed over to the bed where she climbed up on the tall mattress and wrapped her arms around her mother.

"I'm sorry, Mama. I'll try harder to be a better princess." Emerald's voice was tiny.

"Emerald?" the queen said, startled. "Oh no! You weren't supposed to . . . Did you hear all of that?"

Emerald nodded timidly and her mother let out a huge gush of air, her shoulders drooping. She gathered her only child to her in a fierce hug and stroked her hair.

"I'm so sorry. I love you very much." She struggled to find her next words. "My mother . . . well you know Grandmother.

She was very strict about the way a queen should behave. She didn't think I'd ever be able to run a kingdom. After I married your father, I thought she'd be proud. It wasn't good enough. Then she wanted me to have a child. When you were finally born, I thought—at last! Yet still she treats me like I'm failing. I try not to do the same to you, but I think I'm failing there too."

Emerald wasn't sure how to respond, so she held her mother even tighter. They sat in their embrace for a long time not saying anything. Eventually they let go and the queen sighed.

Emerald looked at her mother and thought about her godmother's recommendation about compassion. "We'll figure it out, Mama," she said, smiling. "I promise."

Chapter Five

DAYDREAMS AND NIGHTMARES

"Rise and shine!"

Emerald groaned as she felt herself being shaken gently awake by Viola. Maple, who was buried deep within the warm, fluffy bedcovers next to her grumbled and rolled over. She was not a morning imp.

"Up late reading again?" Viola asked, nodding at Emerald's book, which had fallen to the floor.

"Er, yes." Emerald quickly jumped out of bed and stuffed the book deep in the drawer in her bedside table. Viola cocked an eyebrow but didn't say anything. The past few nights Emerald had stayed up reading the book her godmother gave her until the candle next to her bed burned out. She felt guilty absorbing the text on the yellowed pages of the book, but she couldn't put it down. Why was it forbidden to talk about Queen Ellyn?

The last passage she read before falling asleep the night before was playing over and over in her head this morning.

Queen Ellyn faced the mighty dragon with nothing more than a bow and arrow. She was just fifteen years old, but she was determined to save her kingdom. The dragon advanced on her, opening its mouth as it drew close. Queen Ellyn remained steady. She drew her bow and fired.

Maple startled Emerald out of her thoughts as she stirred in bed and grumbled, "What day is it?"

"It is Tuesday and it is nearly time for your first lesson," Viola chirped as she pulled clean dresses out of their wardrobe. "Get moving, young ladies. I brought breakfast for ye both. Hurry and ye might still get a bite in."

The girls scrambled to get dressed and gulp down some hot porridge before scurrying to the castle classroom. Today's first lesson was diplomacy. Emerald liked her instructor, Master Percy, but she found diplomacy incredibly boring.

"So, if you are introduced to the prince of Bengdu, how are you to greet him?" Master Percy jabbed his stick at a spot on a map plastered to the wall.

"Curtsey and offer my hand for him to kiss," Emerald responded, stifling a yawn as her instructor droned on about the proper way to greet royalty from neighboring kingdoms. She could barely keep her eyes open. Her instructor eyed her warily.

Emerald forced a smile and tried to look interested, but suddenly the strangest thing happened. Master Percy's face began to melt like a candle. A drip of it fell and hit the desk in front of her, causing Emerald to yank her hand away quickly. Emerald shrieked.

"Ugh! Master Percy, are you okay?" She stared horrified at the waxy, flesh-colored puddle in front of her. Then she looked back up at her teacher. His once-human face was now scaly and green. A red, forked tongue darted out from between his thin lips. She tried to push her chair away from the desk but found her legs unwilling to cooperate.

"Wha . . . what happened to you?" Emerald gasped. A cold sweat was forming on her back. She looked around to see if Maple saw what was going on. The imp was absorbed in a book in the corner.

"I'll ask the questions around here," the reptilian instructor hissed. "Where is it?"

"Where is what?" Emerald looked hard at Maple, willing her

to look up. The lizard slammed his hand on the desk in front of her. Startled, Emerald turned back to him.

"Don't play coy with me, little girl," he replied, his yellow eyes darting back and forth and his tail flicking. "You know what I want. Where is your father's crown?"

"On his head, I suppose." Emerald looked around for the quickest escape route. How was Maple oblivious to what was happening? "Why do you want it?"

"Not too sharp, are you?" The lizard rolled his eyes. "Why do I want it? Because it lets you see the future."

Emerald's eyes widened in surprise. Her father had a magic crown?

"Of course. Why would he tell a simple princess about the crown?" the reptile muttered. "Well, no matter. You can still show me where he keeps it."

"I don't think so." Emerald took charge of her body, standing up and shoving her desk back at her instructor. It caught him in the stomach. He doubled over but was too quick for Emerald to get away. The lizard grabbed her arm with cold fingers and dug in tight.

"What did I say about asking questions?" The lizard glared at her. "If you don't help me, I'm going to eat you bit by bit. Starting with this arm."

He opened his jaws, revealing a set of razor-sharp teeth. Saliva dripped from the corner of his mouth onto her skin. Emerald shrieked.

"Maple!"

The little imp didn't even flinch. How was she so oblivious to what was doing on? Emerald looked around desperately for something to defend herself. Nothing. Just books and paper. Her quill had fallen to the ground, out of reach. She wished she had Queen Ellyn's bow and arrow. What would her great-grandmother do in this situation?

The lizard's mouth drew closer and closer to her arm. She could feel his hot, rancid breath on her skin. Emerald squeezed her eyes shut. She steadied herself for the piercing pain of his fangs meeting her flesh. This was it.

"And if you are introduced to the princess of Curelia?" the lizard instructor asked.

"What?" Emerald's eyes shot open. She found herself staring at her instructor whose lizard appearance had miraculously returned to normal.

"I asked how you would act if you were introduced to the princess of Curelia."

"Curtsey and offer my hand for him to kiss," Emerald replied a bit shakily, trying to calm herself down. Maple, who was still in the corner reading The History of Medina and snacking on grapes, snickered. Oh, now she's paying attention, Emerald thought in annoyance.

"The princess? You would give your hand to a princess to kiss? Emerald, you are a million miles away today," sighed the elderly teacher. He ran his hands through his grey hair as he regarded the princess with concern on his face. Was she getting sick? He'd heard rumor of a bad illness making its rounds in the kingdom. "Let's finish our lessons early today," he said gently. "I think you could use a little fresh air."

Emerald looked up, startled. "Really? I mean, yes . . . yes, I could absolutely use some fresh air. I promise I'll study extra hard tonight! C'mon, Maple!" Emerald slammed her Book of Common Courtesies closed and raced out the door before her instructor could change his mind. Maple was close on her heels.

The instructor sighed again and slowly straightened up the desk where they were studying before making his way to the king's chambers. He knocked on the intricately carved oak door that closed the chambers off from a large hallway and gave his name to the page who announced his arrival and let him in.

"Percy!" exclaimed the king warmly, embracing the man who had once been his own tutor. "I'm sorry we haven't had much time to catch up lately. We've had some trouble between our human and magical residents."

The king began pacing and running his hands through his thick red hair. Streaks of white were becoming visible in the king's normally vibrant mane.

"Seems some of our human residents don't like their neighbors from Eseland," continued King Argos in a voice rife with stress. "They've been demanding we shut the border again. You think everyone would be used to each other by now. Our humans don't trust the magic crea—Creatures? Folks? Not really sure what is the proper word to describe them. They aren't actually human, now are they?"

"No, sire," Percy acknowledged. "Perhaps 'citizens' would be a more appropriate term?"

"Hmm." King Argos furrowed his brow in thought. "Yes, that might just work. Citizens! Thank you, Master Percy. You always know just what to say. They don't trust the Eseland citizens because they are different, which they say is bad. Makes my head hurt trying to think of how to make peace between everyone. But listen to me ramble. How can I help you, man? Give me some good news. How's my darling daughter doing with her studies?"

"Well, sire, she is bright and picks things up very quickly," Percy responded.

The king nodded proudly.

"Normally she is an industrious student," Percy continued. "Today, well, today she seemed very distant. It got me thinking—sire, forgive me, but there's rumor of a sickness going around. Many believe the, erm, citizens of Eseland brought it."

King Argos cocked a furry red eyebrow and Percy added quickly, "It's probably nothing. Perhaps a bad night of sleep. And I don't mean to alarm Your Majesty. I just thought it might be prudent to have the royal physician pay her a visit. Just to ensure nothing serious is going on."

"Emerald, sick?" King Argos said, looking panicked. "Clancy!" he called to his page. "Clancy, get the queen. And the physician. And find Emerald. Right away!"

"I'm sorry, Your Majesty," Percy said worriedly. "I didn't mean to frighten you. It's probably nothing."

"Yes, er, yes," the king responded, distracted. "You are dismissed."

The instructor turned to leave. "Oh, Percy," King Argos said suddenly. "Thank you."

Percy nodded and headed out the door. He hoped he was wrong about Emerald being ill. The sickness that was going around the kingdom had taken many lives. If Emerald became its next victim, the king and queen would be devastated.

Chapter Six

A Royal Inspection

Emerald dragged her feet as she made her way to her parent's chambers. Was she in trouble for her lessons ending early? Percy had told her she could go outside. Still, maybe she should have tried harder today.

Maple prodded her friend playfully, trying to cheer her up as they slowly walked through the castle halls. "Look at the bright side—at least you didn't get eaten by a giant lizard."

Emerald groaned. "I almost wish I had."

"That's silly," Maple responded. "Anyway, what's the worst they could do?"

"I don't know!" Emerald fretted, clenching and unclenching her sweaty hands. "They could take away my horse or . . . or . . . or send me to live with my grandmother!"

The two of them shivered. The queen's mother wasn't exactly what you'd call a warm person. She visited the castle once a year to inspect how her granddaughter was being raised. She liked to bark orders and criticize how Emerald and her mother behaved. Emerald would rather be forced to take sewing lessons all day every day than be sent to live with her grandmother.

When they reached her parents' chambers, Emerald asked Maple to stay back. "I should do this on my own," she said nervously. "I don't want them blaming you."

Maple nodded. "I'll wait for you right here." She leaned against the stone wall and slid down until she was sitting.

Emerald gulped and knocked on the big wooden door. It swung open and the princess stepped timidly into the room. "Mama? Daddy?" Emerald nervously uttered. To her surprise, the king and queen jumped from their seats and rushed to her.

"How are you feeling, darling?" the queen asked, putting a hand to her daughter's forehead.

"Are you feverish? Do you feel weak?" The king held his daughter's chin, looking into her eyes.

"I feel, uh, fine," Emerald responded, confused. Why were her parents acting like she was dying? Suddenly she noticed the royal physician in the room. He gestured for Emerald to sit in a high-back wooden chair and began peering into her eyes and feeling her forehead as soon as she sat.

"Master Percy told us he had to end your lesson early," explained the king, plucking at his robes as he watched the physician's examination.

"Oh, well, yes," Emerald admitted. "I fell asleep and had a strange dream that Master Percy was a lizard creature."

"Strange dreams . . . is that a sign of the sickness?" Queen Willow demanded of the physician who looked back up at her, his grey eyes thoughtful.

"It could be. Normally that would be accompanied by fever, though," the physician responded, placing the back of his hand on Emerald's forehead. "The princess doesn't seem to be feverish."

"Wait, it's not! I mean, no—I didn't have the dream last night." Emerald's parents and the physician looked at her as if she wasn't making sense. "I mean, I had the dream—daydream? Daydream during my lesson," the princess explained.

Everyone stared at her. Finally, the physician cleared his throat.

"The princess doesn't seem to have any outward signs of the

sickness going around," he stated. "She does appear a bit fatigued, though. Perhaps an earlier bedtime is in order."

He collected his bag and the king dismissed him. After he left the room, Emerald's parents turned back to her.

"Emerald, what is going on?" the queen gently asked.

Emerald shrugged. "I was up late reading."

"Is that all?" The king was visibly relieved.

"What were you reading?" Queen Willow prodded.

"Um, just a history book," Emerald responded vaguely. She felt the sharp look from her mother's green eyes boring into her.

"Really?" Queen Willow asked, her voice tinged with suspicion. Emerald usually wasn't very interested in history.

"What is the subject of this history book?"

Emerald could feel a guilty look creeping across her face. She wasn't very good at hiding her emotions. "Medina."

Queen Ellyn cocked a graceful eyebrow. "It must be fascinating. Shall I ask Viola to bring it here? I would love to see what history book finally captured my daughter's attention."

Uh oh. Emerald wished she'd brought Maple with her. Her friend was always quicker about talking her way out of situations. For what felt like hours but was only seconds she felt her mother's stubborn patience and her father's bewilderment as they waited for her response. Finally, she said in a small voice, "It's about Great-Grandmother. Queen Ellyn."

The king looked even more confused, but Emerald's mother went pale and sat down abruptly in a second high-back wooden chair near Emerald.

"Godmother gave me the book," Emerald said in a small, submissive voice, then added more passionately, "Mama, why didn't you ever tell me about Queen Ellyn? She was a hero!"

"Yes," Queen Willow responded slowly. "A hero who threw propriety out the window and became the laughing stock of the kingdom." "Is that what you think of her?" Emerald asked, shocked.

"That's what my mother told me about her," the queen admitted. "It's why we don't talk about her. And it's why I don't want you running around with these silly notions that you need to be different. Because you don't. Your job is to marry a prince, have babies, and act as peacemaker for our kingdom. Not to fight dragons."

The king, who had been looking back and forth between his wife and daughter during this exchange, felt his wife's glare and quickly jumped in.

"Yes, as your mother says," he said. "You have a duty!"

Emerald was about to protest when the door to the royal couple's chamber burst open.

"Your Majesties," said a heavily armored guard, dropping to his knees. "I'm very sorry to interrupt. I thought you should know that there's a brawl going on between Master Blacksmith and a centaur. We are trying to control the situation, but other little fights between our people and the, um, others are breaking out."

"Yes, we'll come right away," King Argos said. Both he and the queen moved to follow the guard but were stopped by Emerald jumping up.

"Let me come with you!" she cried, then added as an afterthought, "Please."

The queen's voice was firm. "No, Emerald, you are too young."

"Your mother is right," the king said kindly. "A fight is no place for a child, especially a princess."

"What will you do?" Emerald inquired.

"I think it's time the citizens of Eseland went home," the

queen said softly, looking thoughtfully at the king. He nodded in agreement, though his shoulders slumped at the idea. The royal couple swept out of the room and Emerald stared after them, petrified. What would happen to Maple?

Chapter Seven

A Division in Eseland

"So, are they locking you up and throwing away the key?"

Emerald jumped at the sound of Maple's voice as she left her parent's chamber in a daze. She had forgotten her friend was waiting for her. She looked around for Maple who jumped down from the shoulders of a large ivory statue posing in an alcove in the hallway. It was a nymph draped in flowing garments and playing a harp. *Funny how magical beings are good enough to decorate our hallways but not good enough to live in our kingdom,* Emerald thought grumpily.

"What's eating you, Princess?" Maple prodded her friend. The imp was eating a buttery roll she must have snagged from the kitchen. "Wait—are they sending you to live with your grandmother?"

"No, it's not that," Emerald said, her eyes welling up with tears. "Maple, they're sending everyone from Eseland away."

"What?" Maple's large eyes grew even bigger. She swallowed the last of her roll loudly.

"It's the sickness and all the fighting," Emerald started but Maple interrupted her.

"That's not our fault! It's just a stupid rumor. We can't even get the same sicknesses you humans can!"

"I know, I know!" Emerald cried back. "But the people who want you—the refugees from Eseland—gone are saying the magical creatures are trying to wipe humans out with disease. It's ridiculous, but they're shouting loud enough to make

39

others believe it."

"Are they going to send me away too?" Maple looked as frightened as Emerald felt. Emerald pulled her little friend into a tight embrace.

"I don't know, but I'm going to do my best to stop them."

Hours later, the king and queen found Emerald and Maple huddled together asleep on the bed in Emerald's room. Their faces were streaked with tears. The girls had plainly exhausted themselves crying. The king and queen hesitated to wake them up, but they had to. A decision had been made.

"Emerald, Maple," the queen said softly, gently rubbing their arms. They stirred and groggily opened their eyes to look at her. At first, Emerald felt like she was trapped in another nightmare, but then she shot up straight in her bed realizing that, this time, the nightmare was real.

"What's going on?" she demanded.

"I'm sorry, my dears, but we've had to make a very difficult decision," Emerald's father responded with a deep sigh. "To keep the peace in Medina, we must send all citizens of Eseland home."

"No, but Maple can't . . . she's family!" Emerald cried. She and Maple clung to each other for dear life.

"She is," the queen said sincerely, turning to look into the imp's eyes. "You are, Maple. You have been like family to us from the moment you came to live with us."

"Then how can you send her away? You fight for family; you don't turn them out!" Emerald shouted.

"I'm sorry, my love, but we have no choice," King Argos said, clearly unhappy to be delivering such heartbreaking news. "I wish there were some other way." The look on his face showed just how much he wished he had an alternative solution.

"If I were queen I'd never let this happen!" Emerald bawled, and she and Maple collapsed into tears. Emerald could feel her heart shattering into a million pieces. Maple was the only one who truly understood her.

The two friends clung to each other sobbing as the king and queen looked on sadly. King Argos wrapped his arms around Queen Willow and they held just as tight to each other as the girls did. They knew there was no point in arguing with or trying to further explain things to Emerald. She'd find out one day that ruling a kingdom often meant making difficult decisions.

When the girls' tears finally quieted to sniffles, the queen extracted herself from the king's embrace and moved next to the bed, extending a graceful hand to the imp.

"I think it's best if you gather your things," she murmured, helping Maple off the bed. Maple nodded dejectedly but pulled out a small travel bag from under the bed. She moved around the room as if in a trance, collecting shoes, clothes, and a few personal items. Emerald jumped down from the bed too, glaring at her parents as she moved to help her friend.

"We'll give you two a few minutes, but I think it's best if you say goodbye here," Queen Willow said as she and the king made their way to the door. They glanced back at the girls briefly before closing the door softly behind them. Once they were alone, Emerald turned to Maple who was slowly stuffing what she could of her clothing into a small bag. Her tiny hands were trembling.

"You don't have to do this," Emerald whispered urgently, putting a hand on her friend's arm to stop her from putting a petticoat into her bag. "Just act like you packed. Or do pack. We'll just hide you away. Make them think you left."

Maple looked thoughtful for a moment but finally shook her head. "No, I don't think that's safe. If we were ever caught—Emerald, your people hate mine. I've seen what happens when those in power lose their minds. If they found me, I don't know that they would wait for an explanation."

The imp continued packing her dresses, tears streaming down her face. Emerald stared for a moment, feeling hot anger welling up inside of her. She clenched and unclenched her hands, understanding how that bottle of apple cider she and Maple had stowed in the loft of the barn must have felt before it overheated and exploded loudly into hundreds of pieces, sending the animals into a panic. It had taken Porter all afternoon to round up the escaped horses and restore calm to the stables.

"ARRRRGH!" Emerald screamed. "No, no, no, no, no!" She began pulling out the dresses Maple packed and throwing them on the floor. "I command you to stay!"

Maple looked simultaneously shocked and heartsick.

"Emerald," she began in a tentative voice, which was very unlike the confident imp. This caught Emerald off guard and she froze, her hands gripping the bag that she was preparing to rip up.

"Emerald," Maple began again, hugging the princess around her legs. "I don't want to leave. Not being with you is like not having one of my arms. I'm scared, though. For both of us. If I stay, what would I do? We certainly couldn't run around together like we do now."

"You could hide. You're good at hiding," Emerald tried, but she knew her attempt was weak. The realization that if Maple stayed, she wouldn't really have a life anymore, was slowly dawning on her.

"And what kind of life would that be?" Maple said, echoing Emerald's thoughts. "No, it's better if I go. At least until things calm down."

"It's so unfair! I promise, I'll come for you when I am queen. No one will ever tear us apart again." Emerald collapsed to her knees and wrapped her arms around her friend, shaking and sobbing.

"I hope you can," Maple said. Together, the girls put all of her belongings back in her bag. When they were done, they embraced as though they would never let go. Finally, Maple broke the hug.

"You know, as much as I'll miss you, I think I'll miss the baker's hot cinnamon rolls even more." Maple gave Emerald a crooked smile and kissed the princess on the cheek. "Good bye. I'll see you—and those cinnamon rolls—again."

Emerald watched with a blotchy, tear-streaked face as Maple left the room. Once the imp was gone, she collapsed back on her bed. She felt hollow and empty inside, like a pumpkin that had been cleaned in preparation for carving. She didn't know how she was going to live without Maple.

The next morning, the sun was shining as Emerald strode out to the stables. As bright as it was, she couldn't feel its warmth or light. She was on a mission.

"Porter!" she called loudly as she walked into the stables. The smell of fresh hay and horses enveloped her as she stepped from the brilliance of the outdoors and into the soft light of the horse stable. Her own horse, Allegra, a beautiful gray mare, nickered at the sound of Emerald's voice. Emerald stopped at her stall and the horse greeted her, happily nudging Emerald's hand as the princess petted her.

"Beautiful Allegra," she said softly, stroking the mare's velvety nose. "I'm going to tell you a secret, but you can't tell anyone."

"A secret? This stable has ears, you know," said a deep, gentle voice.

Emerald spun around to find the stable boy she'd been looking for standing behind her. He smiled kindly at Emerald, but there was sadness in his eyes. "I heard about Maple," he said softly. "I'm sorry, Emerald."

"Th-thank you," Emerald responded. She paused a moment to swallow back the emotion that started to choke her up and sent tears into her eyes. "Porter, I need your help."

"Your servant, Princess," Porter said, bowing slightly from the waist. He wasn't mocking her. Emerald could see the sincerity in his brown eyes. She pulled the stable boy closer so she could whisper her plans to him, just in case the stable really did have ears.

"I need you to train me," Emerald whispered. "Really train me. I want to know how to sword fight and shoot with a bow and arrow. And I want to ride my horse like a boy."

Porter considered her carefully. "What about your parents? Won't they be angry if they find out you are training with me?"

"I don't care!" Emerald exclaimed loudly. She glanced around quickly, hoping no one else had heard her. She dropped her voice again and said, "They sent away Maple. I don't care if I never talk to them again!"

"I'm sure that's not true," Porter said gently. "I don't know, Emerald." He sighed. "If we get caught, we'll both be in a lot of trouble. And I don't really like the idea of disobeying your parents."

"Please," pleaded Emerald, tears pricking her eyes again. "I promise we'll be careful. I . . . I need this. Without Maple, I'm nothing."

"That's definitely not true!" Porter exclaimed. He regarded Emerald silently for a few moments before he sighed deeply once again. "Fine. I'll help you. But the rest of the time, you have to behave like your parents want you to. No grief for them. Understand?"

"I understand," Emerald said, grinning at the stable boy and throwing her arms around him in excitement. "You're the best, Porter!"

Chapter Eight

EMERALD'S FIFTEENTH BIRTHDAY

Emerald stared at herself in the mirror. She couldn't believe she was looking at her own reflection. She was wearing her new, long, green silk gown that matched the color of her eyes. Sparkling diamonds and emeralds bedecked her bodice, making Emerald shimmer like a star in the night sky. The young woman in the mirror was so dignified and actually quite pretty.

"Beautiful!" exclaimed Viola. As Emerald's nursemaid since birth, she'd watched the princess grow from a feisty little girl into a lovely young woman. She couldn't be prouder of the princess if she were her own daughter. "Absolutely beautiful. I tell ye, there's not a prince out there who won't be clamoring for your hand!"

"Thank you," Emerald said, flushing. As much as she was dreading her birthday celebration, she was kind of excited about her grown-up wardrobe.

"Now, let me go get your mother," clucked Viola. "I'm sure she'll want to inspect ye before ye go down."

She bustled out of the room, leaving Emerald to continue considering her reflection and the upcoming events of the day. It was customary in Medina for princesses to get betrothed on their fifteenth birthday. Though they wouldn't marry for a couple more years, the betrothal solidified the union between Medina and the kingdom into which the princess was marrying.

Princes from near and far were invited to the weeklong celebration where they all competed in various feats of strength, trying to impress the princess and her family. Emerald had attended her cousin's birthday betrothal celebration a few years earlier and found the jockeying by the princes for her cousin's attention just ridiculous. She'd begged her parents to let her forego her own fifteenth birthday competitions—and to even let her pick a husband later. They refused. Tradition was tradition.

Sighing, Emerald smoothed a loose hair back into her elaborate hairdo. As she did, she felt prickles on her neck, as if someone were watching her. She spun around but didn't see anyone in the room.

"Hello?" Emerald called, uncertainly. Silence answered her. Even though she didn't see anyone there, Emerald couldn't shake the feeling that she wasn't alone. She didn't have time to think about it, though, because her bedroom door suddenly flew open and her mother strolled in.

The queen was dressed in a gown equally elaborate as Emerald's, though hers was blue silk, like the gown she'd worn at Emerald's naming celebration. Queen Willow's best crown, a tiara encrusted with a hundred tiny diamonds, was perched atop her head.

"Oh, my darling, you look absolutely perfect!" Queen Willow said, clasping her daughter's hands and admiring the princess. She gently touched a red curl that was perfectly positioned on Emerald's scalp. "I'll bet you have at least a dozen proposals of marriage before the end of the night!"

"Yes, Mother," Emerald responded dutifully. While Emerald still hadn't forgiven her parents for sending Maple away, she loved them and tried her best to please them, even when it left her feeling all twisted up inside. She'd kept her secrets, though, like training with Porter. Over the years she'd become pretty

proficient in archery, sword fighting, and horseback riding—
something her parents knew nothing about. It often left her
feeling torn inside—acting one way in public but knowing
deep down inside she was miserable and hiding her true self.
She just hoped one day she could reconcile the public and
private Emeralds.

"Well, let's go join your party." The queen held her hand out
to Emerald and the two of them left the room. They walked
in silence down the winding stairs that led to Emerald's
chambers and through the stone corridor that led to the
throne room. Emerald could sense her mother wanted to say
something to her but did nothing to encourage conversation.

When they reached the throne room, the queen kissed her
daughter on the cheek. Queen Willow looked at Emerald for
a long moment as if struggling whether to reveal what she
was feeling, but she finally just wished her daughter luck and
left Emerald to enter the room on her own. The trumpets
blared for the queen's entrance as the doors closed. Emerald
stared at the elaborate wooden doors in front of her. Any
moment, they would be flung open again and she would
make her way down the long aisle by herself. This was the
first time she would make this trek alone. It was a sign of her
becoming a woman.

"Emerald!" The sound of her name made Emerald jump.
She'd thought she was alone in the hallway. Spinning around,
Emerald peered into the deep shadows in front of her. Though
it was lit by torches mounted on sconces and the muted light
of several tall stained-glass windows, this part of the castle
was full of long shadows.

"Emerald, it's me," the tiny voice said again. A small figure
moved out of one of the shadows and Emerald felt her
stomach drop with the shock of seeing the familiar beloved
face in front of her.

"Maple?" Emerald whispered, not believing her eyes. The imp looked exactly the same as she did the day she'd left Emerald seven years earlier. Emerald immediately felt like she was still that eight-year-old little girl spending time with her best friend. It was as though no time had passed at all.

Maple's eyes twinkled and she curtsied deeply to the princess. "Your Highness!"

"Oh, Maple!" Emerald scooped her little friend up in her arms and spun her around. "I'm so happy—Wait, what are you doing here? Did anyone see you?" Emerald looked around her quickly, but they were still alone. She knew any moment now, though, the doors would swing open and she'd have to make her grand entrance.

"I wouldn't miss your big day for the world," Maple said with an impish grin. "Oh, and Eseland is under attack again. But look at you, you look just like a queen!"

"Thank you," Emerald responded, trying to sort out everything her friend said in her mind. "I feel like this is all happening too—Wait, what? You're under attack? What happened?"

"Oh, the evil King Spruce popped up again," Maple said lightly, rolling her eyes like it was a minor nuisance. "And we really need your help. But look at me prattling on. You enjoy your big day. We'll talk later!"

The imp gave her a little shove toward the giant wooden doors to the throne room. They flung open as if on cue. Trumpets blared and Emerald's name was called. She glanced back to look for her friend, but the imp had vanished into the shadows again. Turning back to the throne room, Emerald found herself floating through a sea of both familiar and unfamiliar faces as she made her way up to the throne dais. She tried to smile and look gracious, but all she could think about was Eseland—and her friend—being in trouble.

As she got closer to the throne, she could see her father grinning with pride. Her mother smiled and nodded encouragingly to Emerald.

"You are stunning!" her father whispered to her as she took her place on his right. "You remind me of your mother when she was your age."

Emerald was shocked for a moment as it dawned on her that her father had known her mother since she was fifteen. Then she remembered that she was supposed to meet her own future husband during her birthday celebrations. She shuddered at the thought.

"Daddy," she whispered. "Daddy, I need to talk with you."

"Of course," the king responded, patting her hand. "Let's just get through these formalities first."

"But Daddy—"

"Not now, darling. I promise we'll talk soon." Emerald's father smiled at her dismissively and dropped her hand. Queen Willow gave the two of them a sharp look, then resumed smiling at the crowd.

After a lengthy proclamation announcing the commencement of Emerald's birthday celebrations and her becoming a woman, Emerald had to endure what felt like hours of introductions to royalty and nobility from all of the attending kingdoms. Thankfully she could take her parents' lead on the customary greetings for each. Even with all of her lessons on customs and etiquette, she still felt inadequate to greet so many queens and kings from kingdoms near and far.

At long last, when Emerald felt like her feet would fall off and that the smile frozen on her face might be stuck there forever, the last introduction was made and the guests were dismissed to enjoy refreshments before the first competition among the princes for Emerald's hand.

The royal family retired to the comfortable yet finely

furnished chambers behind the throne room for their own chance to freshen up and take a bite to eat. Emerald decided to take the chance to speak with her parents about Eseland.

"Daddy, Mama," Emerald started as the door closed behind them. Her parents turned around to look at her. Emerald swallowed and continued. "I've come across some information that is rather important."

A knock at the chamber door interrupted her before she could say more.

"Yes?" King Argos called and the door swung open. A messenger for the border guards entered and fell to his knees. "Your Royal Highnesses, forgive my intrusion," he said nervously. He was rather young, Emerald noticed. Probably no more than eighteen or nineteen years old.

"You bring news from the border?" Queen Willow asked.

"Yes, Your Majesty. I'm instructed to tell you that the king of Eseland has returned. He has taken the current royal family hostage. According to what we are hearing, he is putting Eseland's inhabitants under a spell to make them do his bidding. A few creatures have escaped and made it to our border. They say it is bad. Very bad."

"This is what I was trying to tell you," Emerald blurted out. The other three people in the room turned to stare at her. "My, er, source told me Eseland needs our help."

"Is he planning to wage an attack on the human kingdoms?" King Argos asked, turning back to the messenger.

"We don't know, sire."

"Who is your 'source,' Emerald?" Queen Willow asked, though it looked like she already knew the answer.

Emerald froze. She didn't want to give up Maple and get her sent back to Eseland. As if reading her mind, the queen said, "We will keep her safe. We just need to know what she knows."

After hesitating a moment longer, Emerald admitted that it was Maple. The queen nodded, as if that's what she suspected. "We need to hear what she has to say. Please, bring her here. Don't let anyone see her, though."

Before Emerald could leave, though, Maple popped up from under the skirt of a heavily laden table. She was munching on a cinnamon roll.

"Nice to see Your Majesties," Maple grinned, bowing at the king and queen. A small flake from the pastry she'd been eating floated to the ground as she did so. She smoothly brushed it behind her with a quick flick of her foot and an impish smile.

"I hope it's okay that I helped myself to something to eat. I still haven't found any cinnamon rolls anywhere else that taste as good as they do here."

"Maple." The queen nodded, her voice even and her face expressionless. The king, however, smiled warmly and bowed back at the little imp.

"They're right—Emerald and that handsome young man, there," Maple said, winking at the messenger. He blushed deeply. "Eseland needs Medina's help."

"The human kingdoms don't typically interfere with issues in the magical kingdom . . ." King Argos's voice trailed off.

"You can't leave us to deal with the bad king on our own!" Maple suddenly cried with a surprising show of emotion. "Please, Your Majesty, he is trying to control us all. He wants to be the most powerful king ever. He might even come for you next."

"We have to do something," Emerald jumped in, supporting her friend. "It's the least we can do for kicking out the creatures of Eseland all those years ago, and all for the sake of a rumor. It didn't even turn out to be true! The sickness was caused by bad water."

"I don't think now is the time," King Argos said, shaking his head. "We can monitor the situation. Maybe send a peace delegation if necessary."

"Send me!" Emerald demanded. Her parents both looked at her, shocked.

"Oh, Emerald," the queen admonished, "you know that's not what a queen does."

"Queen Ellyn—"

"Enough about Queen Ellyn!" Emerald's mother cried. "You are not Queen Ellyn. You don't know how to wield a sword or bow and arrow. And you certainly don't know enough about diplomacy to conduct peace talks. Why, you still struggle with the most basic greetings for the other human kingdoms."

Emerald glared at her mother in response. She had hoped no one noticed her following her parents' lead as she received the other royal guests.

"Your mother is right," the king agreed. He turned back to the messenger. "Tell the captain to continue to monitor the situation. After Emerald has chosen a suitor, we'll see how things stand in Eseland. Perhaps we'll even bring her betrothed into the discussions."

The messenger bowed and dashed off. Emerald's parents turned back to her and Maple. Emerald could feel her blood boiling. She was about to explode. Maple put a hand on her arm and faintly shook her head. Now wasn't the time.

"Now, we must join our guests and continue your celebration, Emerald," said the queen. She looked sharply at Maple.

"Please wait for Emerald in her room. Stay quiet and do not let anyone see you."

"Yes, Your Majesty," Maple said, curtseying. She and Emerald shared a look before they all left that said they would be having their own discussion about things later.

Emerald followed her parents to the stands that had been constructed to overlook the archery competition. Thirteen princes would be demonstrating their skills with a bow and arrow in the hopes of impressing Emerald. Once the royal family was settled into their seats, the king raised his hand and a trumpet blared, signaling the start of the competition.

Emerald sighed as the first prince took his position opposite the target. He raised his bow, aimed, pulled the string and back away from the bow, then loosed the arrow. It flew across the field and landed just outside the center ring of the target. The audience applauded politely as the prince bowed and prepared the second of his three arrows.

"He's rather handsome," the queen whispered tentatively to Emerald. Emerald grunted in a rather unladylike fashion but didn't look at her mother. Queen Willow sighed and turned back to watching the competition.

Having seen this exchange between his wife and daughter, King Argos turned to Emerald. "She's not the enemy, you know. Neither of us are."

"Maybe not," Emerald responded, "but neither of you are doing anything to stop the enemy."

King Argos sighed deeply. "When you have your own children, you'll understand the difficult decisions parents must make."

"I'll also let them be themselves," retorted Emerald sharply. She could feel her inner rebel forcing its way out and she really didn't care. She was tired of putting on a show. A few lords and ladies seated near the royal family turned and looked. The king waved his hand and smiled. They smiled back and returned to watching the competition.

"Okay, Emerald. Okay," King Argos said, dropping the subject before it got too heated. He too returned his attention to the princes on the field.

Emerald watched the next few princes without enthusiasm. There was nothing particularly spectacular or talented about their shooting, in her opinion. She could do better.

"You could do so much better," a hushed voice from below Emerald's seat echoed her thoughts. Emerald looked down and, peeking out from the skirt that decorated her chair was Maple. Maple winked at the princess and grinned. Emerald looked around quickly to make sure no one had noticed, but everyone's attention was riveted on the prince currently taking the field. He appeared to be a crowd favorite.

Emerald looked back down at her friend. Maple pointed at Emerald and then mimed shooting with a bow and arrow. Emerald shook her head no, but Maple nodded and her grin got bigger. "Do it," she mouthed. She waved her little handkerchief, clutched it to her chest and then pretended to faint. Emerald caught herself before she laughed out loud. She understood what the little imp was suggesting.

Emerald watched the favored prince aim and hit the target dead on. The crowd went wild.

"Mama, Daddy," Emerald said shyly. "Would it be okay . . . I mean is it appropriate . . . I think I'd like to give him my handkerchief."

Her parents exchanged surprised looks. They hadn't expected their daughter to prefer one of the princes so quickly. Still, they were pleased their daughter wanted to express her interest in the customary way of young ladies in their land.

"Of course, dear," her mother said slowly, although she looked a bit suspicious. Emerald tried to look as innocent as possible. She even flushed a bit under her mother's sharp gaze. Hopefully that would sell her request even more. "I'm pleased one of the young men has caught your eye," the queen went on.

"Er, yes. There's one who might not be so bad," Emerald said quickly. "Thank you." She curtsied to her parents and dashed off before they could ask more questions. The king and queen exchanged baffled looks as she left. What was their daughter up to?

Moments later, Emerald and Maple arrived at the stables laughing and breathless.

"Do you think she actually believed me?" Emerald asked Maple. The imp shook her head.

"No, but she really wanted to. That's why she let it go. Oh, I can't wait to see her face when you show those princes what a real princess is like," crowed Maple.

"Whose face do you want to see?" Porter's voice interrupted the girls. Emerald blushed a bit as she turned to look into his brown eyes. At twenty-three years old, he'd grown from a brotherly stable boy into a handsome young man in charge of all the royal horses. Over the years, Emerald and Porter had grown very close as he risked his job and life at the castle to help her learn how to wield a sword, shoot with a bow and arrow, and ride a horse like a knight.

"My mother's. When I outshoot all those princes," Emerald said shyly.

"Oh, Emerald. When will you stop tormenting your mother? She just wants what's best for you." Emerald pretended she hadn't heard Porter and began patting the velvety nose of her father's horse, which was in the stall next to her. Porter turned and looked at Maple. "I see you've returned. Here to be the imp on Emerald's shoulder?"

"If the shoe fits . . ." Maple replied sweetly. She pulled a bag of sweets out of her pocket and popped one in her mouth. Porter rolled his eyes.

"Porter, could you please get my horse ready?" Emerald pleaded. The stable master looked like he wanted to refuse, but Emerald gave him the most desperate look she could and he relented. He always had trouble saying no to her. Sighing, he beckoned Emerald and Maple deeper into the stable and went off to prepare the princess's horse.

"What am I going to wear? I don't exactly look like a man," Emerald said, eyeing her dress unhappily.

"I've got something for you," Maple said. "Here, hold this." She handed Emerald the sweets bag and scrambled up a ladder to the loft. She soon dropped a pair of the king's old pants, as well as one of his shirts and jackets down to Emerald.

Emerald looked at her friend in amazement. Maple shrugged.

"I hid them up here earlier today. I was hoping you would come back to Eseland and fight the evil king. Figured your parents would say no and that you might need a disguise," Maple said as she climbed back down the ladder. She took the sweets bag back and popped one more into her mouth before offering one to Emerald. Emerald shook her head and smiled. Maple shrugged and put the bag back in her pocket. Together the friends pulled off Emerald's gown and petticoats and she pulled on her father's clothes. Luckily her father wasn't a large man, but they still had to belt his pants rather tightly and cuff the sleeves of his jacket.

The sound of Porter clearing his voice made the friends turn around. He was leading Emerald's horse by her reins and looking at Emerald with a rather strange expression.

"You better cover your, um, hair," he said gruffly. Emerald put her hand to her head and realized her beautiful hairdo had come quite undone in the scramble to change her clothes.

A few pins remained, but most of it was now loose and wild.

"Oh, right!" Maple said, and she scrambled up the ladder one more time before dropping one of the king's formal hats over the side of the loft. Emerald picked it up and began stuffing her red locks under the hat. Maple helped, tucking up pieces Emerald missed.

"Maybe they'll just think you're a prince from the islands," Maple suggested as they looked doubtfully at Emerald's disguise. "They do dress pretty strangely."

Emerald shrugged. "I'll be so fast and good, no one will even notice until I take off my hat."

"That's the spirit!" Maple cheered as Porter helped Emerald mount Allegra. She handed Emerald the princess's bow and arrow. Emerald grinned, kicked her heels, and confidently rode out of the stables.

"Be careful," Porter called after her.

When Emerald reached the archery field, the crowd grew hushed to see a new prince approaching the field on a stunning gray mare. The king and queen looked at each other in surprise. They weren't expecting another prince. The queen narrowed her eyes suspiciously at the horse and rider. There was something familiar about them.

The grandmaster, who was the head of the royal knights and in charge of the birthday competitions, looked sharply at the new arrival. He liked everything in order and hated when something disrupted his carefully organized plans.

"And you are?" he sniffed, disgruntled at having to introduce someone unexpectedly. He added belatedly, "Sire?"

"Em…uh, Emmet," responded the disguised princess in as low a voice as she could muster. She wracked her brain to think of a kingdom that wasn't yet represented. "Prince Emmet from the kingdom of West Arden."

The grandmaster looked disdainfully at Emerald but

nodded at the herald to announce the new entry.

"Ladies and gentlemen, please welcome a latecomer to the competition—Prince Emmet of West Arden," called the herald loudly.

Emerald raised her hand and the crowd cheered. The grandmaster put his hands on her horse's reins.

"Shall I take your horse, sir?" he said through gritted teeth.

Emerald shook her head and pulled the reins back, much to the surprise of the grandmaster, herald, and other princes.

"A showoff, eh?" the grandmaster muttered. "Let's hope you're better at archery than you are at telling the time."

Emerald ignored him and kicked her horse into a gallop, firing at each target full-speed. The first arrow landed perfectly. The second arrow landed perfectly. The third arrow hit the bullseye with such force it drove through the target and stuck halfway through each side.

Emerald reared her horse around and faced the shocked and silent crowd. A drip of sweat ran down from her hat and she quickly brushed it away. She nervously awaited a reaction from the audience. Everyone just seemed to be staring at her.

After what seemed like an eternity, the lords and ladies filling the stands, including her own parents, stood and cheered wildly. Though it wasn't forbidden to use a horse in this archery competition, none of the other princes had even thought to demonstrate such daring skill. Even the grandmaster was clapping, though the look on his face said he'd rather not be.

The herald gestured for all of the princes to gather together, so Emerald slowly dismounted and joined the group. She was several inches shorter than even the shortest of princes.

"I wonder who Emerald gave her kerchief to," murmured the queen to the king as they watched the group line up. The herald would be announcing the winner momentarily, not that anyone doubted at this point which prince that would be.

"Speaking of. Where is she?" King Argos looked around the stands for any sight of his daughter. "I hope she didn't miss Prince Emmet's performance. She might actually be impressed by him."

"Yes, or think him a horrible show off," remarked the queen dryly. The king and queen exchanged a look that said they wouldn't put such an assessment past their daughter.

Back on the field, Emerald was being jostled roughly by a couple of the princes standing near her. One or two others made rude remarks about Prince Emmet showing off, but Emerald kept her eyes forward. They wouldn't be so bold if they knew they'd just been beaten by the princess.

After a brief consultation between the grandmaster and the herald, the herald stepped forward and called in a loud voice, "The winner of our archery competition is . . . Prince Emmet!"

The audience once again went wild. Emerald took a deep bow, taking her cap off as she did so and letting her fiery red locks loose. As suddenly as the cheering had started, it ended in a deafening silence.

The king and queen rose in the stands. Queen Willow was white in the face with shock and fury. King Argos clapped a hand over his mouth, unsure whether to laugh or be upset. The crowd stared back and forth between the royal couple and their daughter. Everyone was nearly on the edge of their seats wondering what would happen next. Finally, the king stepped forward and spoke in a loud voice.

"What a fun little treat from our fair princess," said King Argos heartily, hoping to diffuse any anger before it started.

"Not only is she beautiful, she is a true shot. Perhaps she has even struck one of you fine gentlemen through the heart, eh?"

"Oh Daddy," Emerald muttered under her breath while

doing her best not to roll her eyes.

"After so much excitement, I think it's time for a little refreshment," the king continued. "The picnic tents are open and a delicious feast has been laid out. Please help yourselves. The queen, princess, and I will join you in a few moments." He raised his hand in dismissal and the crowd began to drift toward the delicious smells coming from the big white tents on the lawn.

The princes from the competition stared at Emerald and whispered amongst each other. A few strode off angrily, but the rest just looked a little shocked and confused.

Not really caring about what the princes thought, Emerald turned to guide her horse back to the stables. Porter was already there, though, with Allegra's reins in his hands. He shot Emerald a sharp look that said, "I told you so." She sighed and turned to head toward her family's private tent.

Suddenly, Emerald felt a hand firmly grip her arm. She spun around to find herself face to face with a tall young man with sparkling blue eyes. It was the favorite prince from the competition.

"Nice shooting out there," he said humorously. "I hope your parents go easy on you. It isn't every day you meet a princess who can show up a bunch of spoiled princes."

He bowed deeply to her and then walked away. It took Emerald a moment to realize she was holding her breath and that her heart was pounding. She shook her head to clear it. She must still be feeling the adrenaline from her ride and the anxiety of facing her parents. Still, that prince was kind of cute and his reaction wasn't what she had expected.

"Ugh, cute? What's wrong with you?" Emerald muttered to herself as she continued toward her parents. She knew their reaction wasn't going to be quite so positive.

When she entered her family's tent, her parents jumped

to their feet from the wooden chairs on which they'd been sitting.

"Emerald! What in the world—" the queen started, but Emerald interrupted.

"I won the archery competition fair and square, so I . . . I feel I have won my own hand. I choose to marry myself!" Emerald stood defiantly with her hands on her hips.

"Oh, Emerald," Queen Willow said testily. "Don't be ridiculous. You can't marry yourself. Hopefully you haven't offended all of your potential suitors."

"With luck, maybe one or two of them will stick around." The king chuckled, winking at Emerald before catching a dirty look from his wife. Chastened, he swallowed and took on a serious expression.

"Encouragement is the last thing she needs," the queen grumbled. "Emerald, you need to apologize to each and every one of those princes."

"For what? For showing them what it really takes to be a winner?"

"For making a mockery of what is a very serious occasion for our kingdom!" the queen snapped before taking a breath and sighing. "Don't you see? We are doing all of this for you. We want to know that, after we are gone, you are taken care of—that our kingdom is in good hands."

"Why can't I do that myself?" Emerald's voice rose with each sentence. "I'll be a great queen—the best one ever! I don't need a husband to be a great ruler."

"I know you don't," the queen responded more gently. "But it's never been done before. And besides, it's more than just tradition. You need to have an heir of your own. Someone to pass the kingdom down to after you are gone."

The king watched the conversation between his wife and daughter with silent amusement. If there were any two who were more alike in the room, it was the two of them, even if they refused to see it.

"Fine," Emerald finally conceded. It looked like she'd have to go back to being "public" Emerald. "I'll apologize. And I'll try harder to see if I like any of them. Not making any promises, but I'll at least try to give them a chance."

"Thank you." The queen smiled. "That is a very regal response."

"By the way," the king said. "How did you learn to shoot like that?"

"I . . . uh . . . I . . ."

"Yes"—the queen spun around and fixed her with a steely look—"how did you?"

"Well, you see . . . I just had to!" blurted out Emerald. She flushed uncomfortably and looked back and forth at her parents who were watching her intently and waiting for an answer.

"I suppose if you won't tell us who helped you, we'll have to send away all of our castle staff," Queen Willow threatened darkly. "We can't have traitors in our midst."

"That's ridiculous," Emerald shot back furiously, though inside she was starting to get scared. "Just because someone taught me some survival skills doesn't make them a traitor."

"It does if it puts the future of our kingdom at risk," the queen responded. "And teaching you skills that could make you unsuitable for marriage falls in that category."

Emerald and her mother stared hard at one another, each willing the other to break first. King Argos cleared his throat uncomfortably. Knowing how stubborn her mother was, Emerald started to feel her conscience prick. There was no way she could get everyone in the castle fired for her transgressions.

She let out a long breath. "It was Porter," she admitted,

quickly continuing as she saw her mother's face turn the dark shade of red it always did when she was furious. "You can't be mad at him, though. I made him."

"What else has Porter been teaching you?" the queen asked quietly. Emerald gulped. The quieter her mother became, the more upset she was. She was like a teakettle boiling softly before it erupts with steam.

"Just some horseback riding things . . . and maybe . . . how to use a sword," Emerald said in a tiny voice.

"Have you lost your mind?" the queen exploded. Emerald and the king looked at each other as Queen Willow quickly gathered herself and repeated more quietly. "Have you lost your mind? What prince will want you now?"

"I don't know and I don't care!" Emerald retorted, starting to turn her own shade of angry red. "Any prince who wants to rule with me can rule by my side!"

The queen suddenly sighed, collapsed in her chair, and put her head in her hands.

"We'll continue this conversation later," she said wearily. "For now, it's time you change back into your dress and meet us for dinner."

Emerald stared in surprise that her mother was not going to argue with her more. She wasn't going to try her luck and stick around, though. She turned toward the front of the tent to leave when her mother added, "Oh, and Emerald, please just behave like a princess for the rest of the events. The eyes of many kingdoms are upon us."

"Yes, Mama," Emerald said softly and slipped out of the tent before her mother could say more.

The king stared after his departed daughter and back to his wife in surprise. "That's all? You're going to let her go with a request to behave?" His wife never gave up so easily.

"No," responded the queen. "I'm just buying time. If Emerald isn't going to choose a prince, we are going to choose for her. And as for Porter, he is out of here at the first light of dawn tomorrow."

Chapter Nine

A Proposal

Prince Eustace was a tall young man with brown hair and blue eyes. He was very handsome and was used to the ladies of the court fawning over him. Emerald was a bit wild for his taste, but when the king and queen approached him about getting betrothed to her, he readily agreed. An alliance between his kingdom of Arecia and that of Medina would be beneficial to both. Also, as he was the second in line to his throne, he really needed to marry into a kingdom that would put him first in line to being king.

Emerald's parents cunningly sat him next to her at dinner that night. Though she was determined to not show favor to one prince over another right now, Emerald couldn't help but flush when Prince Eustace flashed her a brilliant smile and took his place next to her at the table. Much to her dismay, her tummy was full of butterflies to be sitting next to the same prince who had complimented her after the archery competition.

"My lady," he said, bowing, his soft lips brushing the back of her hand. "May I?" He gestured at the empty seat next to her.

"Of course," Emerald responded a bit shyly. Prince Eustace gracefully sat down and turned his sparkling blue eyes on the princess.

"So tell me, how does one so fair learn to shoot so well?" he asked, cocking an eyebrow.

"Oh, I don't think beauty has anything to, um, do with it,"

Emerald responded, flustered. She fidgeted unnecessarily with her napkin and utensils.

Prince Eustace chuckled. "Perhaps not," he said with a smile, "but it isn't every day you meet a princess of such beauty and . . . talent."

"Oh, er, right." Emerald could feel her ears burning as red as her hair. "A friend trained me," she admitted, cautiously.

"Indeed. Well, your friend is a good teacher," Prince Eustace said sincerely, raising a glass to toast Emerald's teacher. She shyly raised her own in return. "Perhaps I'll have to train with him—or her—myself."

One of the serving girls came to the table then and offered Emerald and Prince Eustace cuts of juicy turkey. The girl batted her eyelashes and smiled coyly as she served the prince. He simply flashed her a charming and kind smile.

"You're quite popular with women," Emerald remarked. She felt a bit of jealousy creeping up within her, catching her quite off guard. Why did she care if this prince had one or a dozen other ladies fawning over him? You're being ridiculous, she told herself. Now is not the time to start liking one of these silly princes. Still, she could feel her cheeks going pink as if Prince Eustace could read her mind.

"I think that's part of the territory of being a prince." Prince Eustace sighed. "Let's not talk about that, though. Let's talk about you."

The rest of the meal flew by for Emerald. Prince Eustace was charming and kind with all the guests and servants, but he paid particular attention to Emerald. He asked her dozens of questions about herself and it wasn't until the end of the meal that she realized she didn't know much about him. She decided to invite him for a walk through the gardens to see if he would be more self-revealing in private.

"How do you feel about female warriors?" Emerald asked

him as they wandered through the royal rose garden. The sun was beginning to set, sending streaks of red and gold across the sky, and the perfume of the colorful flowers was heavy in the air. It was actually pretty romantic, Emerald thought, despite herself. The perfect setting for a fairytale proposal. She groaned internally. Why was she turning to mush again?

"Female warriors? Such as a woman knight?" Prince Eustace stopped dead and stared at Emerald, his perfectly groomed eyebrows nearly touching his equally coifed hair. It was clearly a topic he'd never considered before. Emerald nodded.

"Yes, my great-grandmother was a warrior," Emerald explained. "She saved her—my—kingdom—Medina—from a dragon."

Prince Eustace nodded slowly. "Did she have a husband?"

"Eventually," Emerald responded and then added proudly, "But even after she got married, she still went to battle for her kingdom from time to time."

"I see," Prince Eustace said thoughtfully. "Well, I suppose a woman can be a warrior if the need arises."

"Yes!" Emerald fairly bounced with enthusiasm. "That's what I've been trying to tell my parents. My friend's—Maple's—kingdom is under attack by an evil king. My father doesn't want to get involved yet, but I told them I would go fight for the people of Eseland."

"You are obviously very passionate about this mission," Prince Eustace said. "I would like to offer my services to go and fight for your friend and her people." He bowed gallantly.

"Your services?"

"Yes, I will be your champion." Prince Eustace puffed his chest up a bit. "After all, when we are married—"

"I'm sorry—married?" Emerald choked, stopping suddenly. Prince Eustace halted as well. Next to her, a fountain gurgled happily, sending a stream of water from the pitcher of a cherub into the basin below. She could feel her heart dropping just like the water falling from the pitcher.

"Yes, I know it's a bit soon, but your parents assured me—"

"My parents assured you what? That I would marry you? No one asked me what I wanted," Emerald said, her voice rising steadily. Slowly the realization of what her parents had done crept over her.

The prince looked abashed. "Oh, I'm sorry. Where are my manners?"

He dropped to one knee and grabbed her hand.

"Emerald Aurora Rose, princess of Medina—"

Emerald yanked her hand from his.

"No, no, no!" she cried, cutting him off. "This is not happening. YOU are not happening."

"But we-I-I thought you knew . . ." stuttered Prince Eustace, looking shocked at her reaction. It was the first time she'd seen him less than confident the entire evening. She spun on her heeled foot and stormed away from the prince as quickly as she could.

Emerald ran all the way to her room and slammed the door. Her heart was pounding in her ears. Her parents had betrayed her. Why else would Prince Eustace be so certain she would marry him? Forget her duties as heir to the throne, if becoming queen meant betraying friends and being forced to marry against her will, she would just let her cousin have the throne. She would go and live with Maple in Eseland. Together they would overthrow the evil king and then be free to go on whatever adventures life threw at them.

Yes, she could do that.

The time had come for her to run away.

Chapter Ten

THE JOURNEY BEGINS

Emerald sobbed angrily as she pulled out clothes from her armoire to throw in her little travel satchel. She eyed each dress critically as she did so. Even the simplest of her dresses were still clearly those of a royal princess. She'd never get far looking like royalty.

A knock on the door startled her. She quickly wiped at her eyes and hid the satchel under her dresses.

"Yes, enter," Emerald called, her voice wavering a bit. She hoped whoever was there wouldn't notice. The door opened a bit and the small form of her friend Maple entered the room.

"Oh, Maple," Emerald breathed, relief saturating her voice. "I'm so glad to see you."

"Are you okay? I saw you went for a walk with Prince Eustace and then I couldn't find you."

"He asked me to marry him—and told me I had no place fighting as his future wife."

"Too bad. He was actually kind of cute." Maple twirled a purple curl around one of her fingers.

"Was he?" Emerald said offhandedly, but she could tell her face was getting warm. She quickly changed the subject. "My parents betrayed me! Prince Eustace assumed I'd marry him because my parents told him I would!"

"Wow," Maple responded, her eyes wide. "What are you going to do?"

"I have to leave. If I stay, I'll be forced to . . . to marry that prince!"

"Where are you going to go?" Maple began to pace, tugging at her purple curls as she always did when she was worried.

"I'm going with you. We can defeat that evil king and live in Eseland and do whatever we want for the rest of our lives."

Maple nodded. Suddenly her silver eyes lit up as an idea struck her.

"What if we went to find your godmother first? Maybe she could help us! She did say you should come to her when the time was right—maybe that time is now!"

"Maple, that is a perfect idea!" Emerald's eyes twinkled excitedly before she realized one small problem. "I just don't know where to find her."

"That's easy," Maple responded with a grin. "Before your godmother left after that fight with your mother, she gave me this guiding stone." Maple pulled a small leather pouch hanging on her neck from under the top of her dress. She dumped an unremarkable stone into her hand. The friends stared at it. "She told me to keep it until you needed it. You rub the surface and whisper the name of the person you want to find and it'll take you there!"

"You are truly amazing. Thank you!" Emerald lifted Maple up and spun her around, the two of them giggling excitedly. After she put Maple down, the imp tucked the stone back in the pouch and handed it to Emerald. The princess slid it over her head.

"Now I just need something to wear. These dresses will never do." Emerald wrinkled her nose at them. "I wonder what Queen Ellyn wore to battle. She probably had her own suit of armor."

"Let's ask Porter for some of his old clothes! He'll probably try to convince you not to run away, but he's always a pushover when it comes to you." Maple batted her eyelashes at Emerald, but her insinuation went unnoticed.

"Oh, Maple! You're a genius, as always!" Emerald grinned. Together she and Maple slipped into the secret passageway to make their way to the stables. They stopped in the kitchen briefly where they stuffed a ripped petticoat with bread, cheese, and dried meat. Maple found an abandoned pair of maid's shoes in Emerald's size, which Emerald gratefully swapped with her own pretty but completely unsuitable shoes.

They then scampered across the lawn behind the castle to the stables. The late afternoon sun was warm on their backs. Leaving after dark would have provided more cover, but they wanted to make some headway in the forest while they could still see. Fortunately, they didn't run into any of the castle staff, everyone probably still off enjoying the celebrations.

When they arrived at the stables, Emerald and Maple poked their head in the door. Porter was checking each of the horses and giving them an afternoon apple snack.

"Porter!" Maple hissed, then called again a little louder when he didn't hear her the first time. "Porter!"

He looked up in surprise, but an expression of suspicion quickly crossed his face. Porter gestured that he'd be there in one moment and then turned back to the horse who was nosing his face and hands, impatient for its apple.

Emerald and Maple ducked into the shadows behind the stables to wait for him. They didn't have to wait long. He soon stomped around the corner, a cross look visible on his face.

"What are you two doing here?" he asked grumpily. "Aren't you supposed to be getting wooed by your future husband, Emerald?"

Emerald looked at Porter in surprise. She'd never heard him talk to her like that. "What's wrong?" she demanded.

"Your little shenanigans, that's what," Porter spat back. "I knew it was a risk. Never should have gone along with your schemes."

"What happened?" Emerald asked, an uneasy chill settling low in her stomach.

"Your parents know I've been helping you—training you," Porter answered shortly before sighing. "They told me to leave. I have to be gone by morning."

Emerald and Maple looked at each other, horrified.

"Oh, Porter, I'm sorry," Emerald cried. "I didn't mean for that to happen. I told them about our lessons, but I didn't think they would punish you. I asked them not to."

Porter shrugged. "What's done is done."

"Where will you go?" Emerald asked, feeling very guilty.

"I have an uncle that lives down near the sea. Maybe somebody in his village needs help with their horses. Anyway, it's nothing for you to worry about."

"You should come with us!" Maple suddenly piped up.

"Come with—what are you two up to?" Porter gave the two friends a sharp look.

"We're leaving," Emerald said simply. "My parents think they can force me to marry Prince Eustace. I won't marry someone who thinks he's going to rule my kingdom while I . . . while I sit home and play dutiful wife."

"He was kind of cute, though," Maple pointed out again. Emerald glared at her and Porter snorted. Maple responded with a nonchalant shrug.

"Emerald, you can't just run away from your problems," Porter began, but Emerald cut him off.

"What do you know? You have freedom! You can make your own choices—decide what you want to eat for breakfast or whether you want to marry." Emerald stamped her foot childishly to make her point.

"I'm also not a prince," Porter remarked, but quickly continued before Emerald could fire back a retort. "Look, I just think it's better to confront your problems. Besides, where are you going to go?"

"She's coming to Eseland with me. She's going to save us from the evil king!" Maple bragged.

"I see." Porter sat on a bale of hay and put his head in his hands, rubbing his temples. "And just how are you going to do that?" He sounded tired. "You are a fair hand at the sword and you can hit a bullseye with the best of them, but you've not practiced on a moving target—or someone who's trying to kill you."

"I'll figure it out," Emerald said stubbornly. "Besides, we're going to see my godmother first. She believes in me even if no one else does."

"I do!" squeaked Maple indignantly.

"Besides you," Emerald said, smiling at her friend. To Porter she said, "Believe in me or not, I need your help. Just a small favor. I know I shouldn't ask after I got you in so much trouble. But I need a pair of clothes from you. Please."

Porter sat silent for what seemed like an eternity, and Emerald was sure he was going to refuse. He finally sighed and stood up. "Come on," he said gruffly. "I think going to see your godmother is a very smart idea." *Hopefully she can talk you out of fighting the wizard,* he thought. Out loud he said, "We'd better hurry, though. They'll probably start looking for you soon. You'd better get out of here while you can."

"Thank you, thank you, thank you," Emerald said. She felt horribly guilty that she was once again putting Porter at risk of getting in serious trouble. This was the last time, though. As sad as she was that Porter was going away, and as dearly as she would miss him, he would be much better off without her.

Chapter Eleven

TRAPPED

After Emerald quickly changed into one of Porter's old shirts and a pair of pants that he'd grown out of years before, Porter escorted her and Maple to the boundary between the castle woods and wild forest beyond. The border was marked by an ancient, crumbling wall that was missing big chunks, making it easy to scramble over. The southern kingdoms had been at peace for so long that no one really worried about fortifying the castle grounds in this area.

The three friends didn't talk during their walk—all were wrapped up in their own thoughts. Emerald was imagining charging in and destroying the evil king. Maple was thinking about when they were going to eat dinner. Porter was having doubts about letting the princess and her imp friend go off on their own. When they reached the dilapidated border wall, they stopped to say their farewells.

"Thank you for everything," Emerald said as she fiercely hugged Porter. "I'll miss you."

"I'll miss you too, Princess," Porter said, his voice oddly tight.

"It's not too late to come with us," Maple said as Porter turned and kneeled to give her a hug. He didn't respond for a moment as though he were considering it. Emerald nodded encouragingly, but Porter shook his head.

"No, you'll need someone to cover for you," he said, decidedly. "I can't believe I'm saying this, but if they ask me where you went I'll tell them you said you were planning to head south."

A thought suddenly struck him. "Do you know how to get to your godmother's house?"

"No, but we've got this," said Emerald, pulling out the guiding stone. It was surprisingly ordinary looking. The stone was a muddy brown color and had a smooth surface as if it had been polished or handled a lot.

"What's that?" Porter peered at it.

"It's a guiding stone." Maple seemed inordinately proud of it. "You tell it where you want it to take you and then, bam!"

"Bam?" Emerald and Porter said in unison, exchanging anxious glances.

"Well, I don't know if there's really a 'bam,'" Maple said. "Maybe a poof? Elyria didn't exactly tell me how it works."

"Well, I guess we'll just have to try it." Emerald held the stone near her mouth and said, "Take me to my godmother."

All three companions held their breath and looked at the stone. At first nothing seemed to be happening, then Emerald could feel her hand tingling a bit under the stone. A slender golden arrow lit up on the stone's surface. It pointed slightly to the right.

"Aww, no poof?" Maple said, her shoulders sagging and her mouth drooping with disappointment.

"Looks a bit like a compass," said Porter, peering at the stone over Emerald's shoulder. Emerald took a few steps in either direction and the arrow responded by changing the way it pointed.

"Seems to work like one too," murmured Emerald. She looked at Maple, who nodded, then spun to give Porter one quick and final hug.

"Good bye and good luck!" Emerald whispered.

"You too," Porter said. He quickly kissed Emerald on the cheek then turned and walked away without looking back.

"He seemed pretty broken up about you leaving," Maple

observed as she and Emerald scrambled over a few fallen stones from the wall and walked deeper into the forest beyond the castle.

"Of course. We're friends."

"Hmm," was all the imp said in response. They lapsed into silence as they made their way over the uneven ground. Vines threatened to trip them every few feet and bushes grew thickly in the shade of tall trees, making the light fade even more quickly as the sun set.

"We sound like a herd of cattle," Emerald mused, listening to the crunch of yet another stick beneath her foot.

"Have you heard a herd of cattle?" Maple asked, surprised. She was a bit lighter on her feet being so small.

"Well, no," admitted Emerald, "but it's what I imagine they would sound like. Maybe we can have a farmhouse and our own herd of cows."

"Oh, I like it," Maple said, grinning. "You can milk the cows and I can churn the butter. And we'll have all the yummy cheese we want! We'll be regular farmwives—without the husbands."

Maple and Emerald laughed at the idea.

"Why not?" Emerald said. "We can do whatever we want to!"

"Yeah," cheered Maple. "Maybe we could start by eating dinner, though."

Emerald looked thoughtfully at the thick canopy of leaves above them. The light was waning, but there was still enough to see where they were walking.

"Let's go a bit farther," she said. "We can make camp before dark. I just want a good head start in case Mama and Daddy send the guards after us."

Maple sighed dramatically but kept walking. Emerald glanced down at her stone as they continued their journey. She hoped she was reading the stone right—she'd never actually used a compass before. She also hoped that, when they reached her godmother, Elyria would understand why Emerald ran, and that she wouldn't send her right back to her parents.

"Do you know how to make a camp?" Maple asked, interrupting Emerald's thoughts. "It's a bit embarrassing not knowing how to survive in the wild, being a wood imp and all, but I've lived in castles all my life. Guess I'm not that great of a sidekick." She added the last comment with a sheepish look.

"Oh, Maple, you're the best of sidekicks!" Emerald stopped and kneeled down to give her friend a quick hug. She then stood back up and looked around them. "I've read a few books that talked about what to do. They recommended finding a water source. And we'll have to make beds from leaves. I don't know how to make a fire, though."

"Neither do I," Maple said. "But at least we don't need to cook our food."

Just as the last streaks of light filtered through the leaves of the trees and as the shadows grew so long they threatened to swallow up the entire woods in darkness, Emerald and Maple came upon a small clearing that edged a babbling brook.

"Looks like this is our spot," Emerald said.

"Oh good, now we can eat!" The imp jumped up and down for joy.

Emerald laughed. "Just a few more moments," she said, looking around for the best spot to set up camp. "We should make our beds first. How about . . . there?" Emerald pointed to a fallen tree on the other side of the stream. Branches from some younger trees hovered about eight feet above it like an umbrella, giving a bit of shelter in case of rain.

"Works for me!" Maple said, bounding across a few stepping stones in the river to the opposite bank. Emerald followed her and together they gathered as many leaves as possible to build makeshift beds. Both the princess and imp took long, deep drinks of cold water from the brook and then sat down on their beds to eat. They enjoyed their simple dinner of cheese, bread, and dried meat in companionable silence. As they did, the last of the light faded and darkness swept across the forest. The sounds of crickets and night peepers filled the air and stars began to dot the sky visible above the clearing.

It took a little getting used to sleeping on the hard ground after growing up with soft mattresses and fluffy quilts, but Emerald found she enjoyed the fresh air and freedom. The leaves were cool and smelled so lovely and fresh that they instantly put the princess at ease.

"Do you ever imagine stories for the stars? Like those, for example." Emerald dreamily raised her arm and gestured at the sky. "I like to think they are seven dancing princesses. They spin around in their pretty dresses and have no cares in the world. What do you think, Maple? Maple?"

Emerald pushed up on her elbows to look at her little friend. Maple was sound asleep, snoring softly in her bed of leaves. Emerald smiled fondly and settled back into her own bed. She patted the small leather pouch under her shirt to make sure her guiding stone was safe. Satisfied, she closed her eyes and relaxed. Lured by the sweet smell of the leaves and the lullabies of the night forest, she was soon asleep too.

"Emerald. Emerald, wake up!" Emerald opened her eyes groggily to see Maple crouched above her, urgently but quietly trying to wake her up. The sun was barely peeking through the trees and it took a moment for Emerald to realize that she was in the forest and not in her four-poster bed.

"Emerald," Maple whispered frantically. "We need to leave. I hear noises. We might have followers."

Emerald listened as hard as she could, but she couldn't hear anything. She wasn't going to disagree with Maple, though. Wood imps had very sensitive ears and could hear much better than humans. Together they quickly dismantled their camp, dumping the leaves from their beds into the water to try to cover up their scent. By the time they were done and Emerald had picked up her pack, the princess could hear the noises too.

"Hurry," Maple whispered.

Emerald hastily pulled out the stone. It was pointing north. "Let's try walking in the creek for a bit," she suggested. Maple looked at the water dubiously. It wasn't deep, but Maple only came up to Emerald's knees so would probably be underwater in parts of the stream. Noticing her glance, Emerald said, "I'll carry you. Jump on my shoulders."

"Now I can see what it's like to look down on a princess," Maple joked. Emerald shot her a look, but the two of them froze as they heard the sound of voices too close for comfort.

"Quick," Emerald hissed, throwing her friend up on her shoulders and handing Maple the small pack of food and her shoes. She rolled up her pant legs and stepped into the chilly water. While it had been refreshing to drink the night before, it was so cold this morning that it almost took her breath away. Emerald took a deep breath and quickly began wading up the creek in the waist-deep water.

The voices of the royal guard grew louder and closer. Emerald could hear the tracking hounds barking loudly. They must be picking up their scent. Emerald began moving faster, her feet slipping over the slippery stones and rocks. She tripped and nearly fell as she painfully stubbed her toe on a large rock.

"Ow," she groaned. Maple gripped her head tightly as she

swayed. "Sorry. Didn't see that rock."

"Um, Emerald?" Maple sounded strange.

"Yes, are you okay?" Emerald asked, still moving as fast as she could.

"We have company."

Emerald swung her head around and Maple gasped as she tightened her grip so she wouldn't fall. One of the castle hunting dogs stared at her. There weren't any guards around him, but Emerald knew they couldn't be far away.

"Shh, good boy," she cooed soothingly, holding out her hand in a peace offering. The dog wasn't fooled. It began barking wildly and Emerald heard one of the guards shout,

"Over here! He's found something."

"We've got to run," Emerald said in a hushed but urgent voice to Maple. She jumped out of the creek, swung her friend down, and grabbed the pack. They darted into the woods and began running, keeping the creek to their right-hand side. Fortunately, wood imps were very fast for their size, so Maple easily kept up with Emerald.

They could hear splashing and crashing from behind them as the dogs and their handlers crossed the creek and began tracking them through the woods. Emerald's heart was pounding. They couldn't get caught now. She put on an extra burst of speed and suddenly she and Maple burst through the trees into a large clearing. At the edge of it was a beautiful waterfall cascading over a tall cliff. The water fell about a hundred feet into a pool of shimmering blue water that narrowed at one end and emptied into the stream that Emerald and Maple had been following. It was absolutely breathtaking. It also posed a problem. The stone was urging them to keep going straight, but the cliff expanded far on either side of the pond, blocking their way forward.

Meanwhile, the sounds of baying dogs and shouting men

drew closer behind them. Emerald could practically feel the hounds' hot, foamy breath on her ankles. She knew that if they didn't find an escape route fast, they would be ensnared. At any second, the blood-hungry hunting pack would burst through the woods into the same clearing. She knew the guards wouldn't let the dogs hurt her, but she wasn't so confident about how they would treat Maple. She desperately looked around for any escape. There was nothing. She could feel her heart sinking with each second.

"What are we going to do?" Maple whispered, staring at Emerald in fright. Emerald shook her head, not knowing what to say. They were trapped.

Chapter Twelve

WORKING IN A TROLL GANG

"We have to climb." Emerald eyed the sheer rock face. She was doubtful even as she said it. There was nothing to hold on to. It looked impossible.

"Maybe there's another way," Maple suggested, scampering off toward the waterfall. Emerald also crossed the clearing and began frantically searching the side of the cliff for anywhere they could get a foothold to climb.

"Emerald, come here!" Maple called. Emerald looked around but couldn't see her friend anywhere.

"Up here!" Emerald looked up. Through the mist at the side of the waterfall, she could barely see Maple. It looked like she had scaled a few rocks to a ledge hidden behind the cascading water and protected from the powerful flow by a part of the cliff that jutted out above it, directing the water away from the ledge. The waterfall itself hid the ledge from the front and the mist took care of the sides, so you had to look closely to notice it was even there.

With a quick glance behind her, Emerald darted over to the waterfall and carefully scaled the slippery rocks. The mist and draft from the waterfall made damp tendrils stick to her face, forcing her to keep pushing them out of her eyes. Each time she brushed hair away, she felt herself waver a little on the moist stone, the action throwing her a bit off balance. She quickly steadied herself, though, and determinedly made it to the top. Emerald plopped down next to Maple, panting, after she pulled herself over the ledge.

"I think this is a tunnel!" Maple gestured into the darkness behind them. Emerald peered into the dimness of the hollowed-out space behind the waterfall. It took her eyes a few moments to adjust, but she could just make out a small speck of light coming from deep within the cavern.

"Well, I don't think we have much choice," Emerald said.

"And maybe the guards won't find the tunnel. I could barely see you up here."

Together, Emerald and Maple plunged into the darkness. Not thinking about whether she'd actually be able to see the arrow on it, Emerald took the stone out of her pouch and held it up. To her surprise, it began to glow and cast a warm light on the stone walls and floor around them.

The darkness closed around them as they drew deeper into the cave, making Emerald very thankful for the bubble of light cast by her little stone. After walking for a few minutes and hearing no sounds behind them, Emerald and Maple decided to take a short break. They were exhausted from their sprint.

"Do you think we could have a bite of cheese?" Maple asked hopefully. Emerald laughed and began digging through the satchel in search of their remaining provisions when suddenly they heard voices. She froze. Maple sprang up, grabbing the stone from Emerald's hand and hiding it in her cloak.

"Shhhh," she breathed, pulling Emerald down behind a boulder on the tunnel floor until they could determine if the voices came from friend or foe. Whoever was approaching was speaking in a thick accent that Emerald didn't recognize.

"Trolls," Maple whispered. "They're very feisty. I've met a couple of nice ones, but I've also met plenty who wouldn't think twice about biting off your head."

Emerald swallowed nervously and rubbed her neck.

The shadows around the two friends shifted as the light from torches the trolls were carrying spilled over their rock. The voices suddenly stopped and Emerald could hear at least one of the trolls sniffing the air.

"Who goes there?" a deep, gritty voice called out authoritatively. Emerald and Maple looked at each other. Maple was shaking in fear.

"We know yer there. Ya might as well come out or we'll have tuh drag ya out!" another grumbly voice added.

Emerald groaned internally that she hadn't thought to bring her sword. What kind of hero heads out on a dangerous adventure without some kind of protection? There's always diplomacy, she thought to herself. It wasn't exactly her strength, but maybe she could just talk with them. She'd tell the trolls that she and Maple meant no harm and that they just wanted to get on their way. She hoped these were the friendly sort of trolls.

"It'll be okay," Emerald whispered to her friend and tried to give her the most reassuring look she could. She tucked the guiding stone back into its pouch and hid it under her shirt. Before Maple could respond, she stood up and stepped out from behind the rock. Emerald motioned for Maple to stay hidden. "Hello, um, greetings, sirs and madams," she said, though she wasn't sure if there were actually female trolls in the group. They all looked the same to Emerald. They were a bit shorter than her and had bumpy green skin, unruly brown hair, and bulbous noses. "I am Princess Emerald of Medina. I mean no harm. I would just like to pass through this tunnel."

"A princess? Here?" The largest of the trolls, who Emerald assumed was the leader, croaked as it approached the princess. "What brings ya so far from home, little princess?"

"Yeah, and without nobody tuh protect ya," A different troll eyed Emerald hungrily. Perhaps these weren't the friendly sort of trolls.

"I'm going to see my godmother," Emerald responded as calmly as she could. She held her sweaty palms tight to her legs so the trolls wouldn't see them shaking.

"Well your visit is gonna have tuh wait just a little longer then, princess," the troll leader chortled, smacking its lips as it grabbed Emerald's wrist. "First ye gotta pay the toll."

The troll gang started laughing at this.

"A toll," chortled one of the trolls who was shorter and fatter than the rest. "Like we're bridge trolls. Can ye imagine?"

The troll leader shot the fat troll a dirty look and it quickly sobered up.

"What sort of toll?" Emerald asked nervously. "I don't have any money with me . . ."

"No money, eh? Guess ye'll just have to work it off, then," the troll leader chortled as it forced Emerald's arms behind her and began binding the princess's wrists. Maple caught her eye and made a movement as if to stand, but Emerald shook her head as inconspicuously as she could. The troll leader caught her movement.

"Something wrong, Princess?"

"No, I, uh. Itch on my neck."

"And such a pretty neck it is," the troll said, touching it with a rough, wrinkled hand.

"Hey Mavis," called one of the other trolls. So the troll leader was female, marveled Emerald.

"Whadda ya want, Ernie?" Mavis snapped. "Can't ya see I'm busy?"

"Well, we was just wonderin' what ye thought went better with princess—potatoes or boiled turnips?" Ernie asked with a horrible grin. Emerald felt herself go pale.

"I don't know, Ernie," Mavis responded. "What do you

think goes better with annoying troll?"

"Ohhhhhhh," a chorus of troll voices responded and Ernie turned a darker shade of green. Mavis pushed Emerald forward and the trolls parted to let the two of them through.

"You aren't going to eat me?" Emerald asked timidly. Mavis snorted.

"What sort of savages do ya take us for?" she responded.

"That's the very stereotype that forces us to live in caves like this."

"Oh, sorry," Emerald murmured sheepishly. Mavis grunted and continued to push Emerald forward. The troll's torch cast a dim light over the tunnel floor in front of Emerald, but she still stumbled a few times over unseen rocks and uneven parts of the path. They turned off the path leading to the other side of the cave and began making their way down a long dark passageway, walking for what seemed like hours. There didn't appear to be any light at the end of this tunnel. In fact, the change in air pressure and cooler temperatures made Emerald think they were going deep underground.

As she walked, Emerald could hear the rest of the troll gang behind her chatting and joking with one another. She began to wonder about Maple. Hopefully she was safe.

"What are you going to do with me?" Emerald asked, trying to keep the nervousness out of her voice.

"Why, yer gonna dig," Mavis responded as though it were the most natural thing in the world.

"Dig?" Emerald exclaimed, surprised.

"What, ya got dirt in yer ears?" Mavis quipped. "Yes, dig. Them nymphs in Eseland can't get enough tallyweed. Only grows in caves, ya know."

"Oh," Emerald said. "What's tallyweed?" She couldn't remember any reference to the plant in any of her books.

"Ya don't know what tallyweed is?" Mavis asked, her eyes

widening in amazement.

"Well, uh, no." Emerald stumbled a bit but caught herself before she fell. "I guess we don't have it where I'm from."

"Oh. Thought everybody knew about tallyweed. Has healing powers. Nymphs say it keeps their skin beautiful and youthful," Mavis said. "Can't say it's ever worked on me, though." She chuckled in her horrible, grating way. "Where did ya say ye were from again?"

Before Emerald could respond, there was a commotion from the rear of the group. Shouts echoed throughout the tunnel.

"What's going on back there?" Mavis yelled, her gravelly voice echoing off the walls.

"It's an imp and a human!" the response came back. An imp and a human, thought Emerald. One of them must be Maple. But who was the human?

The gang of trolls parted as much as it could in the narrow tunnel and between them passed a tall young man and a little imp girl. The man was brandishing a sword in front of him. Porter!

"Let her go, in the name of the king!" Porter demanded. The trolls around him laughed but let him through. A wave of happiness went through Emerald. She was saved!

Chapter Thirteen

TALLYWEED TEA

Porter bravely walked right up to Mavis and looked her straight in the eyes.

"Let her go," he demanded again.

"Now why would I do that?" asked Mavis, her eyes sparkling. Suddenly, Emerald noticed some movement out of the corner of her eye. A troll standing off to the right of Porter lifted a club in his hand. Before Emerald could scream, it brought it down on the young man's head. Porter collapsed on the cave floor, unconscious. His sword slid across the ground toward Mavis who kicked it disdainfully out of the way. Another troll picked it up.

"How dare you," screeched Maple. The troll who'd knocked Porter on the head scooped her up and put a hand over her mouth. She wriggled back and forth violently but couldn't get free of his strong grip.

"What should we do with them?" the troll holding Maple asked.

"Please, don't hurt them," Emerald begged.

"Take them with us," Mavis said, ignoring Emerald. "We'll make them dig too. If they don't. . . ." She shrugged and slid a finger across her neck. Emerald shivered and Maple's eyes grew wide. Mavis pushed Emerald forward and the entire group continued walking for what seemed like an eternity. Emerald kept trying to look back and see her friends, but every time she turned her head, Mavis pushed her forward again.

Finally, they reached a place in the cave where it widened out and branched off into several chambers. As the trolls entered the center room, they began putting their torches into sconces drilled just above their heads on the cave walls. The collection of torches cast a warm glow on the cave walls and floor and made it possible to see a bit more of the chambers. Though there wasn't any furniture that Emerald was used to, she could tell that boulders had been chipped and worn down into chairs and tables. There appeared to be piles of leaves in the chambers. Those must be their beds, Emerald realized.

"Ya'll start digging at first light," Mavis told Emerald. "Not that ya'll see the sun come up, though." She chuckled at her own joke and pushed Emerald down next to one of the stone chairs. The trolls threw Porter, still unconscious and now tied up, down on the floor across from her. Maple was also tied up and a piece of material was shoved into her mouth. She was put on the other side of the chair Emerald was next to.

"Time for grub," Mavis called to the group. Two trolls ducked off down one of the side passages. Emerald had a chance to look around, now, and counted about ten trolls total, including the two who must have gone for food. She, Porter, and Maple were outnumbered for sure, but perhaps there was some way they could trick the trolls into letting them go.

Emerald heard a little grunt and saw Maple struggling against her bondage. Emerald tried to make eye contact with her friend to get her to stop struggling. She didn't want them getting in more trouble before she could think of a way out of their predicament.

"Quiet, ya," one of the trolls said, kicking at Maple. She went silent but shot him petulant look. Luckily the troll just grunted and walked away. Clearly a little imp wasn't worth his trouble.

The two trolls who left soon returned carrying a big pot and loaves of what Emerald assumed was bread. The rest of the trolls pulled out bowls from the other chambers and lined up for a scoop of whatever was steaming in the big pot. Mavis brought a bowl and a chunk of bread to Emerald and untied her hands. The troll queen then untied Maple as well and removed the cloth in her mouth.

"Eat up. Ya'll need yer strength." Mavis shot them both a stern look. "And no funny business."

Emerald nodded and accepted the bowl. She looked down at it and her stomach churned. It was a soupy grey mess with some unidentifiable chunks in it. The smell was like dirty socks. She hadn't eaten since breakfast, though, so she decided to give it a try. After all, some of the smelliest cheeses were the most delicious. She tentatively dipped a corner of her bread into the bowl and then took a bite. It tasted like dirty socks too.

Sighing, Emerald put the bowl down and gnawed at the bread. It was nearly hard as a rock, but at least it tasted like bread.

"Psst, Emerald," Emerald heard Maple whisper. "Any ideas how to get out of here?"

Emerald shook her head and the two of them quickly pretended to be eating as Mavis shot a suspicious look in their direction. She eyed Emerald and Maple for a moment and they stared back at her innocently. Mavis grunted and turned back to her own meal.

"Where did you find Porter? And how did you find me?" Emerald whispered.

"After the trolls took you, I didn't know what to do," Maple said quietly, eating the grub as though there were nothing wrong with it. Emerald marveled at how her friend could truly eat anything. Maple wiped a bit of grey juice from the side of her mouth with the back of her hand as she continued talking. "Thought I should get help. Didn't think we could fight off a bunch of trolls ourselves. I went back to the clearing near the waterfall, but I didn't see any of your father's guard. So, I raced to the woods and—smack—ran into Porter. He was looking for us. Wanted to warn us your parents had people looking for us."

Across the cavern, Porter groaned on the floor. Emerald wondered how hard the troll had hit him. She didn't see any signs of blood, but he definitely didn't seem to be doing too well.

"We snuck back into the cave and, well, it wasn't hard to find the trolls what with their smell and the noise they were making," Maple continued, wiping her bowl clean with a chunk of bread. "Didn't really have a plan other than to demand your release."

"Thank you," Emerald said softly. "I'm sorry I got you into this mess."

"Well, we wanted adventure, didn't we?" Maple whispered cheerfully. "Can't get much more adventurous than being captured by a group of trolls. Did you want that?" Maple gestured at Emerald's untouched bowl of food.

Emerald smiled and pushed the bowl to her friend. At least one of them would sleep with a full belly.

"Did you tell them who you are?" Maple asked suddenly, stopping mid-bite to look at Emerald. Emerald was confused.

"Yes, I told them I was the princess of Medina," she responded. "They just laughed at me."

"No—I mean who you are to Elyria," Maple said, her hushed voice growing more excited. She put down the bowl and turned as much as she could toward Emerald.

"Elyria? My godmother?" Emerald asked, but Maple was already clearing her throat and waving at Mavis.

"Excuse me! Um, Mrs. Queen Mavis?" Maple called. Mavis swung her head around angrily.

"Whadda ya want?" she growled.

"Oh, just a little thing really," Maple responded sweetly. "I was just wondering if you knew who my friend here is."

Mavis rolled her eyes. "Yes, she's a princess from some kingdom that doesn't even know what tallyweed is," Mavis said sarcastically.

Maple turned surprised eyes on Emerald. "You don't know what tallyweed is?"

"Well, no, I mean I do now, but . . ." Emerald flushed a bit. She would bet there were plenty of other people—her parents included—who didn't know what tallyweed was.

"You are correct, Mrs. Queen Mavis, that Emerald is a princess," Maple said, turning back to Mavis and ignoring Emerald's embarrassment. "Princess of Medina. You might not have heard of her kingdom, but surely you know her godmother. The Wise Woman?"

A sudden silence fell across the trolls and a look of panic filled Mavis's face.

"She's Elyria's goddaughter?" Mavis said, swallowing. "A human goddaughter?"

"Yes," Maple said, smiling triumphantly. "And she's expecting us at her cottage very soon."

Chaos suddenly broke out in the cavern as the trolls began arguing about what they should do. Some started throwing stuff into canvas sacks as if they wanted to run away. Others held up their knives and insisted the best thing to do was to get rid of the evidence. One of the trolls curled up in the corner in the fetal position, rocking back and forth.

"SILENCE," boomed Mavis. The trolls, Emerald, and

Maple alike all froze. Someone dropped a metal bowl and its clatter echoed through the cave like the clash of a dozen knights in full armor. Mavis glared around and everyone gulped guiltily. She then turned to Emerald, suddenly all full of rainbows and smiles.

"Elyria's goddaughter, eh? Well why didn't you say so in the first place?" Mavis said as sweetly as she could with a voice like gravel. "Perse, untie Princess Emerald and her friends," she directed. "They are our honored guests."

After Perse took the ropes off Emerald's ankles, Emerald rubbed them and then jumped to her feet.

"Porter!" She ran across the room to her injured friend. He was still groggy and half-unconscious but seemed to be slowly waking up. Maple joined her momentarily.

"Does anyone have water?" Emerald asked. Mavis snapped her fingers and two smaller trolls brought over an urn of water and a grubby cloth.

"How about some tallyweed tea?" Maple asked. Mavis looked as though she was about to protest giving away this precious resource, but Maple quickly added, "I'm sure Elyria will be glad to know how you helped her goddaughter's injured friend."

Sighing, Mavis nodded to Perse and he ambled away to make the tea. Meanwhile, Emerald dipped the rag in water, squeezed out the excess, and put the cool cloth to Porter's forehead. His eyes fluttered as he tried to focus on the image in front of him.

"Wha . . .Where?" he mumbled.

"Shh," Emerald replied. "Take your time. Everything is okay."

Porter groaned and put a hand to his head.

"Think you took a pretty good knock," observed Maple. "Don't worry. The tallyweed tea will fix you right up."

Though he certainly didn't seem to be in any hurry, Perse

returned in a short while with a steaming cup of hot tea. Emerald wrinkled her nose when she smelled it. It had an aroma of rotting meat. "Smells horrible but works like magic," Maple promised. Emerald nodded at Porter who was now sitting up with his back against the cave to support him. He took the hot cup with trembling hands and, wrinkling his own nose, took a sip. His reaction said it all—it must taste just as bad as it smelled.

"Drink it all and you'll feel much better," Maple urged. Sighing, Porter pinched his nose shut and finished the tea in two big gulps. His face turned a greyish green and he held his fist to his mouth as though he might not hold the tea down. Finally, though, he took a deep breath and smiled.

"Wasn't so bad." He grinned weakly. "My head is already feeling better!"

Relieved, Emerald turned back to the matter at hand—getting out of the cave and finding her godmother.

"Thank you for your help," Emerald said to Mavis sincerely. "I'm afraid we should be on our way. Could I trouble you for to guide us out of here?"

"Of course," Mavis said. "Can't leave now, though. It's the middle of the night. Wouldn't do tuh let Elyria's goddaughter wander around in these woods before sun up. First thing in tha morning we'll set yas on yer way."

Emerald nodded in agreement. She didn't really fancy heading out into the woods in the dark, even if the alternative was sleeping in a cave with a bunch of grumpy trolls.

"First light, then," she said.

"Ya can take my bed," Mavis said.

"Oh, no, I couldn't," Emerald began to protest, but Mavis raised her hand.

"No arguing, princess. Yer our guest. Ya'll sleep in my bed," Mavis said gruffly, gesturing for Emerald to follow her.

Emerald looked down at Maple and Porter. Maple shrugged and Porter waved them on.

"You two go. I'll be fine here," he insisted. Emerald began shaking her head, but Porter interrupted.

"No arguing, Princess," he said softly with a twinkle in his eye. He and Emerald smiled at each other then Emerald turned to Maple.

"Okay, let's follow Mavis," she said. The two of them followed the leader of the trolls into a fairly spacious chamber off the main cave room. They were surprised to find that Mavis had a pretty comfortable looking bed. It was a feather mattress piled high with quilts that, although worn, looked clean. Two big down pillows were perched at the head of the bed.

"Yas should be pretty comfortable here for the night," Mavis said as she turned to look at Emerald and Maple. She shrugged at the surprise on their faces. "It's nice to sleep on something soft after a hard day in the caves," she explained simply.

Emerald and Maple nodded.

Mavis peered closely at Emerald. "I'm guessing yer parents don't know where ya are, do they?" she asked, though it was more of a statement than a question.

Emerald shook her head no.

"Don't keep them wondering too long." Mavis looked thoughtful. "Children don't know what they do to their parents. I have a son, ya know. Harry. Haven't heard from him in almost a year."

"I'm sorry," Emerald said solemnly. If trolls could cry, Mavis looked pretty close to it. Next to Emerald, Maple shifted uncomfortably.

Mavis shrugged again and quickly regained her composure. "Had a fight with him before he disappeared," she said. "Wish I could let him know I'm sorry. Ya'll tell him, won't

97

you? If ya happen to run into Harry out there? I know it's a long shot. Just want him to know I'm sorry."

"Yes, absolutely," Emerald said. Mavis nodded and turned to go out. Over her shoulder she said, "See yas at first light. Sleep well."

After Mavis was gone, Emerald and Maple looked at each other.

"Well that was . . . interesting," Maple said. "I didn't have her pegged as the sentimental type."

"I hope she finds her son," Emerald said, with true concern and a bit of guilt. "And I hope my parents aren't too worried. I should send them a message."

"I'm sure your godmother can help," Maple suggested.

"Now, don't know about you but I'm ready to try out this bed." She jumped into the pile of quilts and stretched luxuriously. "It's actually pretty comfortable."

Emerald slid into the bed next to her and had to agree. It wasn't quite her bed back at home, but it was cozy. She lay her head down on the pillow and, within minutes, was out.

The next morning, she felt herself being gently nudged awake. At first, she thought she was back in the castle being awakened by Viola.

"It's time tuh go, Princess," said Mavis in her gruff voice. Emerald rubbed her eyes and slowly the room came into focus. The ruddy brown of the cave walls was lit by a torch held by a sconce on one wall. Without a window for light, Emerald wondered how the trolls could tell day from night.

"Hope you slept well," Mavis said. "We've got fresh bread for the journey. Best get ya on your way soon if ya want to reach Elyria's by nightfall."

"Are we that close?" Emerald asked in surprise.

"Just about a day's walk I'd say."

Emerald turned and shook Maple awake. "Maple, get up. We need to go."

Maple grunted and rolled over in the bed. "What time is it?" she asked groggily, squinting as she opened her eyes.

"Just past sun up, I'd say," Mavis responded.

"Not sure how you could tell," grumbled Maple. She definitely wasn't a morning imp.

A few minutes later they joined all the trolls and Porter in the main room in the cave. Emerald and Maple accepted hard but hot rolls from one of the trolls. They ate them along the way as they made their way back through the cave. It was a long walk, but finally they emerged into the bright light of the morning sun on the opposite side of the tunnel to where they had entered.

"Here's a couple more rolls for the journey," Mavis said, handing a bag to Emerald. "And some tallyweed in case yas need it. Hope there's no hard feelings."

"Thank you," Emerald said, accepting the rolls and tallyweed gratefully. They'd lost their other bag in the confusion of the trolls capturing them. "No hard feelings. If we see your son, I'll tell him you miss him."

"Thanks," Mavis responded awkwardly. "Good luck."

She snapped her fingers and the trolls spun and marched back into the tunnel. Emerald turned and looked at her friends.

"Let's go find my godmother," she said.

Chapter Fourteen

A Happy Reunion

"Are we there yet?" whined Maple, petulantly kicking a stick in her path. She, Emerald, and Porter had been walking for hours, following the guiding stone. The bread the trolls had given them ran out after lunch and now it was getting close to dinner time.

"Do you see a cottage?" Emerald replied testily. She was just as tired and hungry as Maple, but she was also doubting her ability to lead. Mavis said her godmother's cabin was no more than a day's walk from the cave, but the sun would be setting soon and they still hadn't seen sign of any kind of habitation. She was starting to worry they'd taken a wrong turn.

"Are you using that thing right?" Maple jumped up to try to see the stone in Emerald's hand.

"How should I know?" Emerald snapped, unable to hide her exasperation. "It's not like it came with instructions. Do you want to give it a try?" She held the guiding stone out in an open hand to Maple. Maple eyed it but shook her head.

"Ladies!" exclaimed Porter, throwing his hands into the air. "Arguing with each other isn't going to help."

"I'm just so hungry," Maple cried as she dramatically flopped down on the ground next to the path and flung a little arm over her head.

"You're always hungry," grumbled Emerald, but she and Porter also stopped. She felt bad about her outburst. She wasn't really mad at Maple. She was actually angry at herself.

What was she thinking running off without any experience or the backup of Medina's knights? Maybe she should have tried harder to convince her parents to let her help Maple and to push back her engagement.

"It looks like we're going north," Porter said thoughtfully, looking around at the trees and sky.

"How can you tell?"

"Well, the sun for one thing." Porter pointed at the fading golden light visible through the canopy of leaves above them. "It's setting off to our left—the west—so we're walking north. Most of the moss is also on that side of the tree," he said, pointing in front of them. "Moss mostly grows on the north sides of trees."

"Oh." Emerald was grateful he knew about things like what direction they were moving just by seeing where the moss was growing. She also felt ashamed she didn't know more of that stuff herself. Sure, she'd spent the last seven years seriously training how to wield a bow or shoot an arrow, but what good did that do if she couldn't even find her way to the enemy in the first place? Maybe her parents were right after all. Maybe there were some things a princess or queen just shouldn't do—like run off to fight an evil king without any sort of real plan or knowledge of how to survive outside a castle. She was starting to doubt she was really up for the adventure she'd set out upon. She sighed deeply and kicked a stone.

"I think we have about an hour of sunlight left," Porter observed. "We could keep walking until it gets almost too dark. Set up camp if we need to."

"Yes, that's probably best," Emerald said uncertainly.

"Maple, do you think you can make it?"

"I'll try," Maple said with a dramatic sigh. She pulled herself off the ground and pretended to steady herself. Emerald and

Porter both rolled their eyes.

"Okay," the imp said. "Let's go."

The three friends continued until the path was nearly invisible in the gathering dark. The guiding stone offered some light, but the deepening shadows of the woods felt like they were closing in on them. Plus, Maple had taken to moaning like a dying dog. They did manage to find a few wild raspberries as they walked, but it did little more than take the sharpest edge off their hunger.

They stopped as a stream interrupted the trail on which they were walking. It burbled invitingly and the three travelers fell to their knees and gulped down the fresh, cold water.

"What do you think about camping here tonight?" Porter asked before taking another deep drink from the stream.

"Yes, let's," Emerald responded, storing the stone in her pouch. "Even if we don't have food, at least we have something to drink."

"And I can't make it a step farther," Maple said, theatrically throwing herself on a pile of leaves a short distance from the stream.

Emerald and Porter pushed some leaves together and lay down close to Maple. Exhausted from their experience in the cave and a day full of walking, all three soon fell asleep.

Bright beams of sunlight peaking through the forest canopy woke Emerald the next morning. She stretched luxuriously, enjoying the fresh air and natural light. After the scare of being held captive in a cave and not sure if she would ever get out, Emerald's appreciation of the outdoors had grown enormously. The freshness of a new day also recharged her determination to tackle the challenges ahead. She pushed herself to a sitting position and looked down at her friends, who were still sleeping. Today she would find her godmother's cottage. She wasn't going to let them down.

Emerald quietly stood and walked down to the creek to get a drink of water. She knelt and brought cupped hands full of the cold stuff to her mouth. As she swallowed, she looked up across the creek. The trail through the woods seemed to be intersected by a smaller path—this one dotted with shimmery pink and blue stepping stones. She squinted through the trees and undergrowth to follow the path up to a wooden door attached to a small . . . cottage! A cottage! Was this her godmother's house? It had to be.

Emerald darted back to her friends.

"Porter, Maple! Get up! We're here!"

"Five more minutes," mumbled Maple as she turned over. Porter, however, sat up and rubbed the sleep out of his eyes.

"Where are we?" he asked in a sleep-fogged voice. He looked a little bleary, but Emerald figured it was from sleeping in some uncomfortable spots the last couple of nights.

"My godmother's cottage," Emerald said, impatiently nudging Maple with her foot. "At least I think it is."

"Why dontcha check it out and come get me when you're sure," Maple muttered, covering her eyes with her hands to block out the sunlight.

"Okay," said Emerald. "But if my godmother has food, I'll probably eat first. After all, I'll need the strength to make it back here."

Maple's eyes shot open immediately. The talk of food was all that was needed to spur her to life. She quickly jumped to her feet. "What are we waiting for?" she demanded. "Come on! Chop chop!"

Emerald rolled her eyes and Porter chuckled, but the three friends gathered up their few belongings and jumped across the creek. Emerald got a better look at the cottage as they drew closer. It was pretty but definitely not ostentatious. The cottage was simply constructed of red brick. Beautiful beds of pink, white, and red ranunculus rested under stained-glass windows that were slightly open on either side of the door. A thin ribbon of grey smoke curled from the brick chimney—a sign that the inhabitant was surely home.

Emerald hesitated when they were on the path. "Do you think she'll recognize me?" she asked. "It might be better if she doesn't. What if she sends me right back to my parents? Maybe this was a bad idea."

"Everything will be fine," Maple assured her. "After all, she refused to change you. She likes you the way you are."

Emerald nodded, though not entirely convinced. She took a deep breath and started walking to the door. Maple and Porter hung back a bit to let Emerald greet her godmother on her own.

Emerald paused again when she reached the door. If she was going to turn around, now was the time. No! That was weak. If she couldn't face her godmother, there's no way she could face the evil king. As she stood there her stomach gave a sharp growl. Her empty belly was voting for her to knock—especially with the heavenly scent of baking bread wafting from the open windows.

Taking a deep breath, Emerald raised her fist to knock. Before she could make contact with the door, however, it swung open and out stepped her godmother.

"Emerald! Oh, my dear, I've been waiting for this day for the past seven years," the woman said, tears glistening in the corners of her eyes. "Come in. Please come in!"

Emerald's heart pounded and she considered whether or not she should just turn around. Her godmother seemed pleased to see her, but what would she say when she knew

Emerald had run away?

As if she'd read Emerald's mind, Elyria interrupted her thoughts saying, "Don't worry, my child. I'm not going to send you back to Medina. You have important things to do! Let's start by getting you some food."

Emerald felt a tug on her sleeve and looked down. Maple was standing there grinning up at the two women.

"Maple!" the godmother exclaimed, kneeling and clasping Maple's hands affectionately in her own. "I'm so happy to see you, my old friend."

Porter stepped up next to Emerald. He smiled shyly at Elyria who stood to get a good look at him.

"And who is this?" she asked with a curious twinkle in her violet eyes.

"Porter, ma'am," he said, sticking out his hand. "A friend of Emerald's. Pleased to meet you."

"Porter! I hardly recognize you." Emerald's godmother ignored his hand and stepped past Emerald to give him a big hug. "I haven't seen you since you were a child. You've grown into quite a handsome young man." Porter's face turned a bit red, but he looked happy. After she released Porter, she extended her arms to guide all three friends into the cabin, sniffing a bit as she did so.

"All three of you could use a good scrubbing," she said. "You smell like a troll's den."

Emerald, Porter, and Maple all laughed at this and Elyria cocked an eyebrow.

"Sounds like you've already had some adventures," she said. "You can tell me about them over breakfast."

Elyria gave each of the three travelers a steaming mug of tea before making them scrub in hot tubs of water. She set up a sheet near the fireplace to give each of them a bit of privacy as they bathed. Though she was very hungry, Emerald had to admit she felt much better after she was clean. She sat at a knotty wooden table and nibbled on some fresh, crusty bread while she waited for Maple and Porter to finish their baths. As she snacked, she told her godmother about the trolls.

"Ah, Mavis," Elyria said fondly after Emerald finished her tale. "Her bark is certainly worse than her bite. She's a good egg, though."

Porter and Maple soon joined Emerald and her godmother at the table. Elyria piled their plates full of roast suckling pig, fresh cheese, and juicy strawberries. There was also plenty of fresh bread and butter and icy cold milk to drink. Emerald's godmother watched contentedly as Emerald and Maple tucked into their hearty meals. Porter just picked at his food, though.

"Porter, is everything okay, darling?" Elyria asked.

"He got hit on the head by one of the trolls," Maple said through a mouthful.

"Yes," Porter said. "I have a bit of a headache, but it's better than it was. I'm just not that hungry right now."

"Hmm," said Elyria, but she didn't push him further. She let the three friends continue eating and it was only as they drained the last drops of milk from their cups and were digging into a fresh apple pie that she broached the subject about their presence.

"I'm assuming, Emerald," she began, "that your parents don't know you're here. Is that correct?"

Emerald nodded guiltily, swallowing a big, sweet chunk of pie and piping up defensively before her godmother could respond. "They were going to force me to marry this horrible prince," Emerald said, shoving her half-eaten pie away from her. She was prepared to run if she had to. She was not going back to Medina now. "Well, maybe he's not horrible. But he thought MY kingdom would be his. That he would rule it

AND me. I want to make my parents happy, but I don't want to be miserable."

Elyria nodded sympathetically.

"He was cute, though," Maple piped up.

Emerald shot her a dirty look. "You keep saying that," Emerald complained. "Why don't you just marry him?"

"Maybe I will." Maple stuck out her tongue. Realizing she had a bit of crust on her finger, she licked it off while her tongue was still out. "Then I'll be a princess too."

Porter cleared his throat uncomfortably. "Aww, don't worry, Porter," Maple continued, ignoring Emerald's glare.

"He's got no chance with Emerald."

Elyria glanced at Emerald and Porter, both of whom had turned bright red, and smiled knowingly to herself before changing the subject and saving them from further embarrassment.

"Mothers and daughters have argued about life and love since the beginning of time," she said. "A mother's love is so deep it can blind her. She wants what she thinks is best for her daughter at any cost—even if the price is sometimes happiness. Your mother loves you so much, Emerald. I believe she is wrong that you have to change to be a good queen. But I know she is coming from a good place."

Emerald nodded. "That's why she wanted you to make me more like her."

"Your grandmother was very strict with your mother. She didn't dare step out of line. Your mother tries to go easier on you, but she has a narrow view on what it means to be a princess. When your great-grandmother died, your great-grandfather was devastated. He was determined that none of his female descendants would ever be a warrior again. That worked fine for your grandmother and mother. But you are different. Your story is different."

Elyria stood and collected a steaming kettle from the fireplace.

"Tea?" she asked, looking at each of her guests. They all nodded. She flicked her wrist and four clean clay mugs appeared on the table. She poured a generous serving of tea in each one.

"Cream and sugar?" she offered, snapping her fingers. A cream and a sugar pot danced from a shelf on the wall to the table. Emerald marveled at her godmother's skills and Porter's eyes were as big as saucers. Only Maple seemed unfazed by the magic. Elyria noticed Emerald and Porter's stares and chuckled.

"Simple magic," she said modestly. "I don't use much these days. Not since, well . . ." Her voice trailed off and she looked hard at Emerald for a moment before continuing. "Emerald, dear, I think you coming to me now is fate nudging you in the right direction."

"What do you mean?" Emerald took a sip of her tea. It was warm and spicy and instantly made her feel relaxed.

"Have you heard about what is happening in Eseland?"

"I told her," Maple piped up. "She's going to help save the kingdom."

"If I can," Emerald mumbled, staring into her cup.

"I believe you can," Elyria said. "But you need to know what you are up against."

Elyria waved her hand again and suddenly the flames in the fireplace began to separate and dance. As Emerald looked closer, she could see them start to form images. Suddenly she could see a handsome young elf king, his beautiful nymph wife, and a cute little girl. Next to Emerald, Porter gasped. Once again, Maple was the only one unfazed.

"Fifteen years ago, right about the time you were born, Eseland was a happy place," Elyria began. Emerald could see the flame images holding hands, spinning in a circle and laughing. "But the king and queen had a terrible secret. Their daughter, Raina, was born without magic. This frightened the king and queen. They were afraid their daughter would be banished like so many other children. So they made a deal with a powerful troll named Harry."

"Mavis's son," Emerald interjected, tearing her eyes from the scene in the flames to look at her godmother in surprise.

"Yes, Mavis's son," Elyria responded, taking a sip of her tea. "He's a good troll—if a bit misguided. If you save Eseland, you might just save him too."

No added pressure, Emerald thought apprehensively as Elyria continued the story.

"Harry enchanted a stone that gave Raina magical powers." The flames shifted again, showing a troll offering a small object to the little child. "He meant well by it. Unfortunately, in the wrong hands the stone was incredibly dangerous.

"A few months after Raina received the stone, strange things started to happen." The flames flashed angrily and showed scenes of chaos and panic among the magical creatures of Eseland. "Spells went awry. Wands turned up missing. There were reports of wolves and ravens gathering together and running military drills. Rumors spread about an evil power getting ready to attack."

The flames now showed a frightened crowd of creatures marching into the throne room of an elaborate castle. "The inhabitants of Eseland confronted the king and queen with their fears." The fire characters took over for Elyria, acting out the story.

"We think it's Harry—the troll. Ever since you brought him back, so many bad things have happened," a short gnome cried out. *"Just last week he gave my wife a weird look and now she has a wart growing on her nose. A wart!"*

109

There were a few snickers around the room; the wart on the advisor's wife's face wasn't new. It had been growing there for some time.

"Yes, yes," sighed the king. "We hear all of your concerns, but we still think there has to be a perfectly logical explanation for what is happening. A group of crows is always creepy—it's called a murder! As for the wolves, prowling is what they do. It probably just looked more organized than it really was."

"You just don't want to admit that you could be wrong about the troll . . . um, sire," piped up a young imp, who swallowed nervously after his outburst. The king sat in shocked silence and his lack of comment fueled the bravery of a few others.

"We should call in the Wise Woman! She'll know what to do."

"Absolutely not!" exclaimed the queen, slamming her slender hand down on the edge of her throne, startling everyone in the room. Up to that point she had been silently observing the debate. "As the king said, there has to be a perfectly good explanation for what is happening." She added coldly, "Do any of you want to question us further?"

There was a rumble of disgruntled murmurs throughout the room, but no one said anything else. The meeting disbanded and the king and queen retired grumpily to their chambers.

Elyria's voice broke back in, continuing her narration as the flames continued to morph into new scenes. "A few days later, the first case of a person losing their magic powers was reported. Frightened crowds once again mobbed the throne room, demanding a response."

"Young Jamie was turning into a talented elf!" shouted an elf woman from the fireplace. "He could make anything grow with a wave of his wand! And he could talk with animals! Now, plants turn brown at his touch and any animal that sees him runs away in fright!"

"Now, now," the king said. "Do you have proof that he was ever

magic in the first place? Let him show us what he can do with plants and animals."

The boy's mother looked at the king, confused. "Sire, I just told you, he lost his powers. How can he show you what they used to be if he doesn't have them anymore?"

The king shook his head sadly. "Then we have no way of knowing if you are telling the truth."

"But I know him too," piped up one of Young Jamie's neighbors. "He helped me with my garden, he did!"

"I also know him," cried a young elf girl. She blushed as she continued. "He used to help me talk with my pet rabbit. It was really sweet!"

The queen held up her hand and said, "We don't know exactly how magic works. Why some are born with it and others aren't. Maybe it sometimes fades as we age. It may be scary, but we can't change the way things are. Now, leave us!"

Elyria picked up the narration again. "Once again, the crowd dispersed unhappy and unsettled. They couldn't understand why the royal couple was turning such a blind eye to what was happening in their kingdom.

"Over the next few days, more and more cases were reported of elves and fairies losing their powers. The king and queen still refused to discuss what was happening with Eseland's inhabitants. Eventually they barred the way into the castle and banned all but a few select servants and Harry.

"As more and more creatures lost their powers and the castle refused to get involved, the people of the kingdom decided to take matters into their own hands. A committee of two fairies, two elves, and one young imp who had lost his powers was nominated to go visit the Wise Woman."

"That's you!" Maple piped up. Emerald jumped. She'd been so absorbed in the story and the apparitions in the fireplace, she'd almost forgotten where she was.

"Yes." Elyria smiled. She took another thoughtful sip from her teacup and offered more of the hot beverage to Emerald, Porter, and Maple. Emerald gratefully accepted another cup of tea.

"They came here, risking their very lives crossing Ortland," Elyria said when she was satisfied that everyone had the refreshments they needed. "They begged me for help."

"Please, Mother, our magic is disappearing. The king and queen won't help us. You are our last hope," cried a young fairy from the flames in the fireplace. Her frail shoulders shook as tears ran down her pale face.

"I listened to their tales of disappearing magic," Elyria continued, "then I promised to go and speak with the king and queen myself." She turned to the desperate fairy in the flames. "Don't worry. Whatever is happening, I'll get to the bottom of it."

"I followed the villagers to the castle," Elyria went on.

"When I got there, the guards refused me entrance. I had to use a little, ahem, influence to get in."

In the fireplace, a miniature version of Elyria waved her wand. With a loud crash, the castle gates flung open. The guards who had been blocking her way landed, stunned, on their bottoms.

"I am going to see the king and the queen," the pint-sized Elyria said, stashing her wand again and smoothing her wild curls. The guards stared at her, wide-eyed, but did nothing to stop her. She strode through the courtyard, passing beautiful rose gardens and gurgling fountains without so much as a glance. At the end of the courtyard was a grand marble staircase. The mini Elyria seemed to float up them to the massive wooden doors. The doors were barred tight, but Elyria once again brandished her wand and flung them open.

When she stepped inside, the castle was eerily quiet and

unusually dark. Obviously not bothered by the ambiance, Elyria strode purposefully to the throne room and shoved open its ornately carved wooden doors. Here, too, it was shadowy and silent.

"Well that's odd," murmured miniature Elyria. "Where has everyone gone?"

There was a slight scurrying noise that caused her to turn sharply toward the heavily curtained windows. She pulled out her wand, which illuminated, and pointed it toward one of the deep red curtains, which was still moving gently.

"You there, show yourself!"

The youthful face of a wood imp girl in a maid's cap timidly peered out.

"Maple, that's you!" Emerald cried, shocked. She didn't know why she was so surprised, though. She knew the imp had lived in castles all her life.

"That's me." Maple grinned. "I don't think I've aged a day since then."

Maple's fire replica spoke. *"I'm sorry,"* she squeaked. *"I shouldn't be here. Please let me go."*

"Don't be afraid. I won't hurt you," Elyria's fiery likeness responded.

"No, but they might!"

"Who might, dear?" Elyria's eyebrows shot up.

"I can't. I've said too much." Maple shook her head and made as if to duck back behind the curtains. Elyria approached her slowly and held out her hand to the shaking imp.

"No one is going to hurt you," Elyria said softly. "Please at least tell me where the king and queen are."

The imp raised her arm and pointed up but didn't speak.

"The tower?" Elyria asked.

The imp maid nodded and then scurried off.

"I climbed up the winding stairs to the tower," the real Elyria broke in. "Along the way, I didn't see any other castle staff. When I reached the top, I could hear voices from behind the door to the room at the top."

"But how are you doing it? I demand to know," came the voice of the king from the fireplace. The Elyria lookalike was pressed up against the door listening.

"Ah told yah, ah can't tell yah. It's too dangerous!" responded a second voice in a deep, gritty tone.

"I don't care what you told me," shouted the king. "I want to know how this stone works. How does it take away powers?"

Suddenly, there was the sound of scuffling from behind the door. The miniature Elyria grabbed her wand and threw the door open. She froze at the sight.

The flames morphed into the king wrestling with the troll. The queen was cowering in the corner with her arms tightly wrapped around Princess Raina. Elyria's entrance startled everyone in the room, so much so that the king and the troll crashed to the floor.

"Harry! What on earth are you doing?" Elyria demanded as she held up her wand and gestured toward the king. "King Spruce, quick, get behind me."

"Ah don' think—" started the troll, but the king interrupted him. "Oh, Elyria! Thank goodness you are here! Harry has been threatening us and our kingdom."

Elyria regarded the troll sternly as she held her wand at him. The king, meanwhile, made his way across the room and cowered behind the Wise Woman.

"Harry, what sort of mischief are you up to now?" Elyria asked disappointedly. "I thought you learned your lesson the first time you messed with dark magic."

"Ah did," Harry responded, glaring at the king. "But he convinced me tuh help him. He said he just wanted tuh help his daughter. Instead he wants tha power fer himself!"

"What?" Elyria spun to face the king, shocked. He held up the

enchanted green stone, which began to glow. Suddenly she looked weak.

"Harry, what have you done? What did you create?" Elyria gasped, falling to the floor.

"It was just meant tuh help tha princess have some magic," responded the troll, miserably. "Ah never thought her daddy would steal it fer himself."

"Your highness, King Spruce, this isn't you!" Elyria pleaded. She turned to the queen and her daughter. "Queen Ivy, surely you can do something!"

The queen shook her head. She seemed to be entranced by the light of the stone.

"We will rule all," Queen Ivy said mechanically as she smoothed the sandy-blonde hair on her daughter's head.

The king held the stone higher and the light grew stronger.

"She has power. Power we want. Power we need," the king chanted, pointing the stone at Elyria. The light emitting from it was dazzling and Elyria started to walk toward it, drawn by some unseen power.

Suddenly, Harry pushed Elyria out of the way. She rolled and landed with a thud against a wooden desk. It was topped with glass vials that wobbled precariously at her impact. Thankfully they all stayed upright, saving Elyria from a shower of glass.

The troll tackled the king. They rolled and tumbled with lots of grunts and groans. Then Harry seemed to gain the upper hand and he rolled on top of the king, pinning him down.

"Drop tha stone now," grunted Harry, straining with the effort of trying to hold down the wriggling king beneath him.

"Never!" cried the king as he suddenly wrenched the arm holding the stone free. With his other hand, he grabbed a silver pot that had fallen to the floor during the fight and brought it down on Harry's head with a sickening crack. The troll slumped down on the king who somehow still managed to wriggle free from Harry's

thick, hairy body.

Elyria pushed herself to her feet, but the king was already looming toward her. The stone began to glow even more powerfully as the king raised his voice and roared, "We don't just want her power. We want her life!"

Elyria drew her wand and tried to cast a spell of protection, but it was no use.

"I could feel my powers draining from my body," Elyria said from the table back in the cottage. "Everything was growing dark. I knew I was done for."

"What happened next?" breathed Porter. Now over the shock of a fireplace theatre, he was clearly enraptured by the story.

"It was strange. As suddenly as I felt my power leaving me, I also felt it returning," Elyria said. "When my eyesight was restored, I saw Harry grasping King Spruce and swinging him around. The stone flew out of the king's hand and sailed across the room. It seemed to move in slow motion. Then"— Elyria paused, seeing the scene replay in front of her eyes even though she wasn't looking at the fire—"then it hit Queen Ivy in the head. I saw her slump to the ground. I knew it was over."

Emerald, Porter, and Maple stared at Elyria in silent horror. They all jumped this time as a voice screamed from the fireplace.

"Mama. MAMA!"

In the flames, little Raina had crawled out of her mother's arms and was pulling on the queen's dress urgently. She was sobbing, not understanding why her mama wasn't answering her.

"Ivy, my darling, my love, are you all right?" the king shouted fearfully. Harry, keeping a strong grip on the king, nodded to Elyria to check on the queen. She walked over and knelt next to Queen Ivy, gently touching her neck and hands.

"She was gone," Elyria said, sadly.

The queen might not have been innocent, but Emerald was sorrowful that she had been killed. She could feel her heart breaking for the little princess. Her mourning was interrupted by an utterly animal sound from the chimera king as he sank to his knees. The little princess looked from her father to mother in confusion and then ran, bawling, to her father for comfort.

"The king was defeated," Elyria recounted. "I took away his wand and used the stone to revoke his powers. It felt strange to pull the magic from another being. Almost seductive. I had to get it out of my hands as quickly as possible. I shoved it in a big wooden box, locked the box, and handed it to Harry. Then I ordered him to guard it with his life as punishment for creating such an abomination."

"What did you do with the king?" Emerald breathed.

"I took King Spruce and the poor princess to live in a distant region of Ortland." Elyria's voice was filled with pain. "I didn't want to punish Raina, but I thought it would be worse for her to live without her father. As much soul as he lost stealing magic from others, I knew the spirits of Ortland would leave him alone. And I knew he wouldn't let them touch his daughter. I couldn't risk letting him live near civilization—magic or human."

Emerald stared at her godmother in amazement as the woman finished the story. Porter looked equally as incredulous.

"Your godmother saved us all," Maple said as she turned adoring eyes on the old woman, who smiled back at her kindly.

"But if you took the king's powers and banished him, how did he come back?" Emerald asked, suddenly confused about the recent change of events in Eseland.

Elyria sighed. "I thought—hoped—King Spruce had learned his lesson and would live out his life in peace.

Apparently, however, he got a taste for power. And he just couldn't get that taste out of his mouth." She stood and began clearing up the dishes. Having seen how she used her wand before, Emerald wondered if Elyria's actions were more to keep her hands busy than really needing to do work.

"I believe Harry might be involved again," Elyria admitted as she poured hot water into a shallow tub on her counter and began washing dishes. "I haven't heard from him in months. Somehow King Spruce must have tricked Harry into giving him back the stone. Rumor has it, Spruce turned his replacement king and queen into stone and is trying to force their son to marry Raina."

"Could I help you with those?" Emerald pointed at the dishes. She'd never washed anything other than her face, but she was willing to give it a try. Elyria shook her head and smiled kindly.

"I appreciate it, child," she said. "I like working with my hands, though. It reminds me to be grateful for the life I have and the little magic I have left." She dried her hands after rinsing the last cup and turned back to Emerald.

"If you are willing to face the king, it won't be easy." Elyria looked intently at her goddaughter. "Many magical creatures have tried to face him, but all have been destroyed. It is rumored that only a hero of pure intent—one who isn't driven by the desire for power—can stop him."

Emerald stared back as a feeling of uneasiness crept down her back like the prick of a dozen little icicles. "I want to help, but I don't really think I'm a hero. I'm definitely not Queen Ellyn," she admitted.

Porter and Maple, who had been silently observing the conversation, both looked as though they wanted to speak, but Emerald raised her hand to stop them. She knew how her friends felt. She wanted to hear what her godmother would say.

Emerald's godmother smiled at her. "My dear, this is what you were born for. I see a lot more of Queen Ellyn in you than you realize. She, too, didn't think she had what it took to be a hero."

"Maybe," Emerald said doubtfully. "But, I mean, you'll go with me, right? With your magic powers and my, well, 'pure intent,' we can defeat him together!"

Elyria shook her head sadly. "I would if I could, but I never fully recovered from the first time he tried to drain my powers. I'm afraid if I go up against King Spruce again, I won't have the strength to battle him." She walked over to Emerald, put her hands on the princess's shoulders, and looked deep into her green eyes. "No, you must face him alone. You have what it takes to defeat him. No one must ever have such power again."

"You can do it, Emerald," Maple agreed, coming around the table to hug her friend. "I know you can!"

Emerald was more than a little doubtful. But she had a lot of people counting on her. More than that, if she succeeded she might be able to show her parents that she was meant to be more than just wife to a prince.

"I suppose I could try," she said dubiously.

"No, Emerald, this is crazy." Porter jumped to his feet. "We should go back and get help from your parents."

Emerald regarded Porter. He had a good point, but if she went back nothing would change. This might be her last chance to prove herself.

"No," she said firmly. "I'm going."

Chapter Fifteen

THE GIFTS

Emerald stretched luxuriously in the trundle bed in her godmother's house. It wasn't anything fancy, but after spending the past few nights on piles of leaves and in a cave, the trundle bed felt heavenly. She turned her head and saw her godmother was already up and was cutting thick slices from a fresh loaf of bread for their breakfast. Next to her, Maple stirred, snuggling a bit deeper into the pile of patchwork quilts that covered them, as if unwilling to give up the warmth and coziness yet.

"Good morning, Maple," Emerald murmured.

"Morning," Maple mumbled back, squeezing her eyes tight against the light beginning to seep through the cracks in the shutters.

Hearing the girls stirring, Emerald's godmother turned to them and said, "Oh good, you two are up. Come get your breakfast while it's hot and ready!"

She's awfully cheerful for someone about to send her goddaughter into imminent danger, thought Emerald grumpily.

As if reading her mind again, her godmother added, "You're going to need your strength for what lies ahead of you. But I have faith that you will succeed."

The front door of the cottage swung open and Porter entered carrying a load of firewood. Elyria nodded at him and pointed to the corner next to the fireplace.

"Please put that over there," she said. "Thank you. Breakfast is ready."

Porter dropped the load of firewood where Elyria had directed him. He was pale and sweating. Emerald looked at him with concern, but he shot her a teasing smile and said, "Planning to sleep all day?"

"No, I'm getting up." Emerald flushed as she spoke. "Turn around, please. I need to get dressed."

Porter obeyed and Emerald rolled out of bed. Her leather trousers and white shirt were resting on a chair next to the trundle. They were both now clean, thanks to her godmother. She pulled them on and put her leather pouch back around her neck as Maple also rolled out of bed and dressed.

"Okay, we're decent," Emerald said, and she and Maple joined her godmother and Porter at the table for a feast of savory sausages, perfectly fried eggs, and hot bread.

"Now," her godmother started after they'd all helped themselves to heaping plates of the food. "Your guiding stone will help you find the kingdom of Eseland, but first you must cross the marshes of Ortland. Be careful there. The marshes are boggy and unforgiving and full of the souls of the human and magical creatures who got lost there."

Porter and Emerald exchanged nervous glances while Maple shivered and went pale.

"You've crossed Ortland a couple of times, haven't you?" Emerald asked Maple. Maple nodded.

"Yes, it's horrible." Maple shuddered. "But I think I can guide you through it."

"Thank you, Maple," Elyria said in a voice full of pride and appreciation. She smiled at the imp reassuringly and then continued. "When you get to Eseland, you'll find King Spruce and Raina in a small cottage just outside the castle grounds. He is about appearance as much as he is about power. He wants it to look like he is marrying back into the kingdom. Doesn't fool anyone, of course, but it might be a weakness you can use to your advantage. Still, you must be careful of him. He is sly and cunning and can be absolutely charming when he wants to. Destroy his source of power and you destroy him."

"And how do I do that, exactly?" Emerald asked, swallowing a mouthful of sausage. "Destroy him, that is. I don't have weapons. Even if I did, I don't think they'd be any good against an evil, magical king."

Porter took this as an opportunity to add his own objections. "She's right, you know," he said. "Emerald's just a child, she shouldn't—"

"I'm not just a child," Emerald said, her voice suddenly full of resolve. "I can do it. I just need some suggestions how."

Her godmother cocked an eyebrow and then suddenly shot up, one finger pointing straight in the air as if she just remembered something. "I have a couple of gifts for you," she said, making her way over to an ornately carved wooden trunk under one of the front windows. She pushed open the lid and began rummaging through what appeared to be piles of clothes and blankets. Finally, she emerged with an oblong bundle swaddled in an old but clean blanket. She undid the wrapping to reveal a bow with a golden grip and a leather quiver full of golden arrows. Everyone stared at the beautiful instrument.

"This belonged to Queen Ellyn," said Elyria. Emerald's green eyes grew even wider. Suddenly, she was full of questions, but she didn't know which one she wanted to ask first.

"So you knew her? This was really her bow and arrow? And, forgive me, but . . . how old are you anyway?"

Elyria laughed. "Yes, I knew her well. She was a dear friend of mine and made me the godmother of her first child—your grandmother. I've been godmother to the princesses in your family for three generations now." She chuckled and added, "As far as my age, well let's see . . . I'll be 125? No, 126 next month."

She handed Emerald the bow and arrows and Emerald reverently turned them around in her hands, admiring the fine workmanship. Tiny flowers etched into the golden grip cascaded from the top to the bottom like petals falling from a cherry blossom tree. The arrows were slender but very strong and had fine feathers at the tail end. The nocks were plated in the same shimmering gold.

"It's beautiful," she gasped.

Maple and Porter crowded around Emerald, murmuring their admiration and running their fingers along the bow.

"Quite," Elyria agreed. "Queen Ellyn would be so proud to see you with her prized bow and arrows. Of all her talents, archery was her best—and favorite—skill."

"Just like you," whispered Maple. Emerald felt a shiver run up her spine. Maybe her godmother was right—she was who she was meant to be.

"Just one more thing, my dear." Elyria turned to the mantel and began rummaging through a smaller version of the wooden chest. "Ah yes, here it is." She returned to the table and slipped a small silver ring adorned with a pink stone on the fourth finger of Emerald's right hand.

"Keep this safe with you," Elyria said. "If you are ever in trouble, rub your fingers over the stone and ask for help. It will provide you with what you need." She hugged Emerald tightly and added, "I wish there was more I could do for you, but alas, this is a journey you have to complete on your own."

"As for you two," Elyria said, turning to Porter and Maple. "Emerald is going to need all of the support you can give. Watch over her. Help her when you can. But know there are difficulties ahead that she will have to face on her own."

They nodded solemnly.

"Porter, take this flask. Even if you can't find a stream, it will always be full enough to quench your thirst," Elyria instructed, handing a metal flagon wrapped in leather and hanging by a leather strap to the young man.

"Yes, ma'am," Porter looked at the flask in awe as he took it. He uncorked the lid and took a sip. "It's cold!"

Elyria chuckled and turned to Maple. "For you, Maple, I have a whistle. Blow it, and no matter where I am, I will know you need me." Elyria gave her a small silver whistle on a yellow cord.

"Thank you," Maple responded, humbly accepting the gift. "You don't also have a sack of never-ending food, do you? 'Cause we got awfully hungry on the way here."

"That I do not have," Elyria said, smiling fondly at the imp. "But I'll send you with enough provisions for a few days. When you get to Eseland, you should be able to get help from a small contingent of creatures who haven't been enchanted by the king. They'll do their best to make sure you are prepared for the remainder of your journey."

After that, things moved very quickly. Emerald, Porter, and Maple finished their breakfasts while Elyria filled a sack with some apples, bread, cheese, meat, and a couple of blankets. Before she knew it, Emerald was saying goodbye to her godmother.

"Believe in yourself and you will succeed," Emerald's godmother assured her as they embraced one more time. "I know you can do this."

"Me too," piped up Maple as she grabbed her friend's hand. Together, the three friends walked back into the woods to face Emerald's fate. As they walked, Emerald shot several glances back to her godmother's cottage. A sinking feeling at the bottom of her stomach warned her that she was beyond the point of no return. Life was going to change for her forever. She only hoped she had the strength to face it.

Chapter Sixteen

ORTLAND

Emerald, Porter, and Maple followed the stone north all day. The sun was beginning to set as they finally emerged from the woods and found themselves at the border of Ortland.

"We should stop here for the night," Maple declared. "The marshes are scary enough. I don't want to be wandering through them after dark."

"I'll get some wood," declared Porter.

"Take the stone," Emerald said as he turned to leave. "That way you can find us when you are done." Porter nodded and accepted the stone before setting back off into the woods behind them.

"Let's see if we can find a good spot to sleep," said Emerald. "It doesn't look like it's going to rain, but I don't exactly want to be sleeping next to the marshes either."

Emerald and Maple began investigating the area at the edge of the woods. There was a small stretch of open grass that separated the marsh from the line of trees. While the ground there would certainly be softer, it wouldn't offer the same sense of security as keeping a couple of trees or rocks between them and the marshes.

"How about here?" Maple asked, pointing at a small clearing behind a boulder just inside the tree line.

"Perfect!" Emerald said. "I like having something solid between us and the bog." She paused and stared back at the marshes apprehensively. "It feels like we are being watched."

126

Maple shivered and drew closer to her friend. "I know."

Together they created three makeshift beds of leaves and pulled out some of the food Elyria had given them when they left her.

"Emerald? Maple?" Porter's voice drifted over to the two girls at their camp.

"Over here!" called Emerald. She stood up and waved, though in the gathering darkness she couldn't really see anything. She was greeted by silence. "Porter?" Emerald called uncertainly. She listened, but there was no response. "Porter?" she called again. Suddenly, Emerald felt a tug at her sleeve and she nearly jumped out of her skin.

"Sorry," said Maple in a hushed voice. "Didn't mean to scare you. Where is he?"

"It's okay," Emerald replied. "I guess I'm a little jumpy. He stopped responding. I think I should go look for him. Hopefully he didn't wander too far . . ." Her voice trailed off, but both she and Maple knew she was alluding to Porter getting lost in the marshes. "Stay here." Maple was about to protest, but Emerald stopped her. "We can't both go and risk all three of us being separated. Wait and see if he turns up. I'll just go that way," she said, pointing into the woods where Porter's voice had come from. "I'll be back in ten minutes. If I'm not, well, use the whistle and call my godmother."

Maple nodded and turned around to grab Emerald's bow and arrow. "Okay," she said, "but at least take this."

Emerald accepted the bow and arrow gratefully. Though she had no idea what might be out in the woods, it made her feel better that she at least had her great-grandmother's weapon with her. She began to make her way deeper into the woods in the direction she'd last heard Porter.

"Porter!" she called every few steps, pausing to listen for a reply. "Can you hear me?"

She stumbled through the woods for about five minutes before it became nearly impossible to see. Emerald knew she couldn't go much farther without a source of light. Soon she wouldn't even be able to make her way back to camp.

All of a sudden, she heard a groan. It sounded like an animal in pain. Her heart began to pound. She hoped it was Porter and not some wild beast. Just in case, she nocked an arrow and held it half-drawn, prepared to shoot.

"Porter?" she hissed, pointing her bow in the direction of the sound. "Is that you?"

"Emerald?" A feeling of relief flooded Emerald's body as she lowered her bow. Porter's voice was weak, but Emerald could follow it to her right.

"Keep talking to me so I can find you," Emerald instructed, her heart slowing to a normal rate.

"I don't know what happened," Porter said feebly. "I was fine and then I blacked out."

"Probably still affected by the hit you took from the trolls," Emerald said as she felt her way carefully through the thick undergrowth, trying not to stumble on Porter. She nearly fell over him, though, as she pushed between two thick and prickly bushes.

"Ow!" Emerald rubbed her arm where she caught it on a thorn. She knelt down with her hands out to find Porter at her feet. "Here, let me help you up. Do you think you can walk?"

"I think so."

Emerald helped him sit up. "Good. I'll take the wood. We have some tallyweed. Maybe we can make you some more tea when we get back."

"Ugh." Porter shivered.

"I know it's pretty nasty, but it's all we have," Emerald said practically. "Maybe you just need more than one dose to get better."

She helped Porter to his feet and gathered up his bundle of wood. Together they made their way slowly back to camp, using the guiding stone for a bit of light.

"Oh, there you are," exclaimed Maple as they emerged into the small clearing near the rock. "I was about to call your godmother."

"Porter's still a bit woozy," Emerald explained, dumping the wood down and helping him sit with his back against the rock.

Maple tilted her head and studied him. "Poor you," she said.

"I can make you some tea—" She frowned as she realized that they had the materials they needed, but not the know-how to actually build a fire.

"I can talk you through it," Porter said weakly.

"I'll do it," Emerald said, eager to learn a new skill. Maple shrugged and sat down to watch.

"Take the small sticks and separate them from the bigger ones." Porter pointed at the bundle of firewood he had gathered before fainting. Emerald did as instructed, kneeling next to a small fire ring Maple had constructed with stones while she was gone.

"There should have been an old nest in the wood pile. That's your tinder." Emerald looked around and located a small bird's nest that had fallen unnoticed from the pile of wood.

"You're going to need a flat piece of wood and a stick with a sharp end." Emerald and Maple looked through the pile of wood until they found pieces that met Porter's approval.

"Okay, now put a bit of the nest into a notch in the bigger piece of wood." Emerald tucked a bit of the dry grass and twigs that formed the nest into a hole in the larger chunk of wood. "And put the sharp end of the smaller stick on top of that. Now twist it between your hands until you see a spark or smoke." With the last bit of instruction, Porter closed his eyes and lay back, exhausted.   Emerald swiveled the stick between her hands with a furrowed brow. Drops of sweat formed on her forehead as she worked. It didn't feel like she was making progress, but she was determined not to give up.

"You can do it," whispered Maple, impressed by the effort Emerald was making. Emerald kept rotating the stick though her arms soon felt like they were about to fall off. Just when she thought she was going to have to give up, she saw a small puff of smoke and a glowing ember.

"Fire!" she yelped, almost forgetting to keep turning the stick. She looked up at Porter to ask him what to do next, but his eyes were closed.

"Maybe put it in the fire ring with some more nest and twigs?" Maple suggested. Grateful for any kind of assistance, Emerald followed Maple's recommendation. Luckily the embers caught and soon she had a little fire going. She slowly added a bit more kindling and a few small branches to the blaze, careful not to extinguish it.

"You did it," Maple said in awe.

"I did." Emerald wiped her brow as she stared at the flames. Maybe she could do this adventure stuff after all.

"We don't have a tea pot," Maple said, breaking into Emerald's thoughts. "But I did find this." She displayed a bowl-sized rock that had been worn down in the middle so that there was a space where liquid could sit. "It's not deep enough to boil the water, but maybe if I heat it enough and let the leaves steep, it'll help a little bit."

She gave it a try. Once the water was steaming, the imp added a couple of the tallyweed leaves to the water and let them soak for about five minutes. Meanwhile, Emerald roused Porter.

"Nice fire," he said. Emerald felt her face growing warm, but she brushed it off as being from the heat of the flames.

"Here, drink this." Maple handed Porter the rock bowl. He made a face but obediently drank it. He then ate a little food and lay back down to go to sleep. Emerald tucked one of the blankets around him.

"I'm worried about him," Emerald said, studying her sleeping friend. "Maybe we should have left him with my godmother."

"You know he wouldn't have stayed," Maple said, shooting a knowing look at Emerald. "He thinks it's his duty to protect you."

"I know." Emerald sighed and then changed the subject. "You and I should take shifts tonight. I don't like the feel of it here."

"They say the spirits of those who were lost in the marshes walk them every night." Maple shivered and pulled her woolen cape closely around her. "I don't think they should bother us here, but I think you're right. I'll take the first shift."

Grateful once again that her little friend had decided to follow her, Emerald lay down, wrapped herself in the other blanket, and fell into a restless sleep. The moon was high in the sky when she woke later to take over the watch.

It was unnaturally quiet. No owls hooted and no breeze moved the trees, yet as Emerald stood and stretched she could swear she saw the marsh grasses swaying hypnotically beyond the boulder. She shook her head and closed her eyes, trying to refocus. It had to be an illusion. She opened her eyes again but the grasses still seemed to be swaying in the thick mist that quilted them. It was almost mesmerizing. Emerald could feel herself being lulled into a trancelike state. She didn't know why she'd been afraid. It was really so peaceful.

She moved a little closer to the marshes without realizing

what she was doing. One foot after the other, as if she were floating. It was so easy. Her next step would take her into the bog. She lifted her foot. Suddenly, she felt something pull her hands, knocking her off balance. She fell backward onto a small form who let out an "oof!"

"Maple?" Emerald snapped back into consciousness.

"What were you doing?" Maple's voice shook in terror as she and Emerald untangled themselves from each other.

"I don't know. It was so peaceful. I felt drawn to the marshes." Emerald stood and offered a hand to her friend. Together they stared back at the now motionless marsh grass.

"The spirits were trying to pull you in." Maple's eyes were enormous. "That's how it happens. They pull you in and never let go. We have to be very careful. Let's stay awake together tonight."

"You saved me," Emerald said shakily. She couldn't believe how close she'd come to making a fatal mistake. "Thank you." She knelt and hugged her friend. "I don't know what I'd do without you."

It was too dark to see, but Emerald sensed Maple was blushing. The two of them returned to their camp and found Porter there still sleeping peacefully.

"Let's not tell Porter," she suggested, still shaking. "I don't want him to worry."

Maple agreed. Then the two of them huddled together the rest of the night, counting down the minutes until the first light of dawn.

Chapter Seventeen

THE MARSH SPIRITS

Emerald startled awake the next morning to the harsh cawing of a murder of crows. She and Maple must have fallen asleep at some point the night before. Emerald couldn't see them, but the birds' cries came from the direction of the marshes. A feeling of unease ran down Emerald's spine like a stream of icy cold water.

"Do you hear them too?" Maple asked, nearly making Emerald jump out of her skin.

"Oh! Yes. It's pretty spooky," Emerald responded, her heart still pounding. She looked over at Porter. He was still sleeping, oblivious to the racket. He was curled up in a ball and was breathing shallowly. The dark circles under his eyes seemed even more pronounced in contrast to his sallow skin. "He doesn't look good," she said.

Maple glanced at Porter and frowned. "Maybe a little breakfast will perk him up."

"Perhaps," Emerald said, not really convinced.

Together she and Maple assembled a quick breakfast from the few ingredients they had. Maple boiled some more water for tallyweed tea and Emerald roused Porter. He slowly rose from his bed of leaves and looked around a bit groggily.

"Did we find your godmother's cottage yet?" he asked.

Emerald and Maple exchanged worried glances. "Yes, we left there yesterday," Emerald responded gently.

Porter looked a bit confused. "Oh," he said, rubbing his

head. "I must be more tired than I thought."

"Here, drink this," Maple said, handing him the makeshift rock bowl. It held a bit of steaming liquid in the center of it. Porter accepted the beverage and drank it.

"Shouldn't that be working by now?" Emerald whispered to Maple, indicating the cup.

"I think so," Maple whispered back. "I've never seen a human take it before, though."

"Hey, ladies!" Porter exclaimed. "My head is fuzzy, but I can still tell when my friends are talking about me."

"We're just worried about you—that's all." Emerald handed him a bit of cheese and bread. "Here, eat this."

"Thanks," Porter said, accepting the food. He hungrily took a bite. "I'll be fine. I'm just hungry and tired."

"Maybe you two should stay here—let Porter rest," Emerald said.

"No!" Porter and Maple both exclaimed at once. Maple stood and faced Emerald with hands on her hips.

"Absolutely not," she said stubbornly. "You are not going into Ortland by yourself." Emerald shot a quick glance at Porter and then scowled at Maple. Maple glared at her but simply added, "I'm staying with you."

"Look, Porter's in no condition to go with us—and he can't stay here alone," Emerald said, standing up and putting a small hunk of the remaining cheese and bread in her bag. "Use your whistle and call my godmother for help. Please? For me?"

Maple and Porter looked as though they wanted to protest again, but both decided against it seeing the stern look on Emerald's face.

"Fine, but don't do anything stupid," Maple said, giving her friend a hug so tight it was as if she'd never let go. "Okay?"

"I'll be very careful," Emerald said, squeezing her friend

back. After they broke their embrace, Emerald kneeled next to Porter and gave him a hug too.

"I'm supposed to be protecting you," he grumbled.

Emerald smoothed a lock of hair back from his forehead.

"And I'm supposed to be protecting you," she said, smiling.

"Get better so we can celebrate the defeat of the evil king." Emerald sounded a lot more confident than she felt as she uttered that last statement.

"Here, at least take this," Maple said, holding out the flask to Emerald.

"No, you might need it—"

"Take it. No arguments." Maple was adamant. "Now, get going. You'll need a full day to cross the marshes."

Emerald gathered up her bow and arrows and slung them across her shoulder. She tucked the flask in her little bag of food and put it on her opposite shoulder. After giving each of her friends a final hug, she began walking towards the marshes.

"Whatever you do, stay on the path," Maple called from behind her. "And don't listen to any voices."

Emerald turned and gave her friend a nod and wave, then swallowed, took a deep breath, and kept trudging forward.

In the morning light, the Ortland marshes looked almost peaceful. A narrow path cut through long, yellow-green tendrils of grass that came up to Emerald's shoulders. The rising sun cast a warm glow on the landscape. As she walked deeper into the marshes, the land quickly swallowed her up. As far as she looked in every direction, she could see nothing but the vast sea of vegetation.

The guiding stone pointed true and took her across solid ground, but if she looked to either side, Emerald could see where the path dissolved into murky, foul-smelling water. Though she couldn't see anything in it, Emerald could swear she felt something watching her from the watery depths.

"I can't imagine anyone living out here," she said out loud, breaking the silence of her determined march.

"Weeeeee do," a voice hissed in response. Emerald looked around wildly but didn't see anyone. She thought of Maple's advice and didn't respond. She quickened her pace, hoping to get away from whatever was out there.

"Come, join us," the voice continued. "It's so lovely in here."

Emerald shook her head and picked up speed, trying to block out the voice. A mist slowly wafted through the marsh grasses toward her. It floated onto the path and swirled to surround her. There was no escaping it. Every which way she turned, Emerald could see the creeping fog.

Tendrils of the mist began wrapping around Emerald's feet and legs. It was cold as snow but not unpleasant. Emerald felt like her body was slowly falling asleep. No matter how hard she tried to struggle against it, she couldn't fight the numbing sensation. Soon she couldn't even walk. She was frozen in place. Emerald groaned. She couldn't be defeated this quickly. Oh, if only she had a horse—then she could ride out of here.

She began to rub her hands together nervously, a couple of fingers brushing the ring her godmother had given her. She looked down at it. What had her godmother said? Rub it and think about what you most need and it will come to you?

Emerald squeezed her eyes shut and began stroking the ring and thinking as hard as she could of a horse. She could feel the numbness up to her waist now. Hopefully this ring answered requests quickly.

As the cold sensation began to near her chest, she heard a thump and a whinny. Emerald's eyes flew open and, standing before her, to her amazement, wasn't just a horse. It was a . . . "Unicorn?" Emerald gasped in wonderment. She'd heard stories about them before, but, to her knowledge, no human had ever actually seen a unicorn. It was breathtakingly beautiful with hair as pure and white as snow and a horn on top of its head that shimmered and changed color as it moved. A pair of gossamer wings adorned either side of its muscular body. The unicorn nodded to Emerald.

"Quick, get on!" Its voice was as smooth as vanilla ice cream. It kneeled down on its front legs in front of Emerald so she could grip its mane and swing herself up onto its powerful back. The lower half of her body was stiff, so Emerald struggled to pull herself up. Sensing this, the unicorn extended one of its wings and gently guided the princess onto its back.

The unicorn quickly took flight and Emerald held on as tight as she could to its silky mane. As they rose away from the mist, she could feel the sensation coming back into her lower body like the pins and needles you get if your leg falls asleep. She looked down and found herself a bit dizzy to see the landscape flying by below them. Emerald buried her head in the unicorn's mane.

"Everything okay back there?" the unicorn called back in its silky voice.

"Just a bit dizzy," Emerald answered, still unable to push her head up from the unicorn's back.

"Happens to nearly everyone their first time flying," the unicorn consoled her. "Unless they were born to fly, of course."

Emerald appreciated the unicorn's effort, but her heart was still up in her throat. She began to take deep breaths and after a few moments, her heartbeat finally began to slow. She was also able to adjust her legs for a better grip on the unicorn now that she could actually feel them again.

"Thank you for saving me," Emerald said when she could finally lift her head and open her eyes.

"You're welcome," the unicorn responded. "I found you just in time. A moment or two longer and you would have been lost to the marsh spirits."

Emerald stole a tentative look back down at the ground below them. Luckily this time she didn't get nearly so dizzy. She couldn't believe her eyes. Ortland was massive. The marshes stretched as far in every direction as she could see.

"Incredible," Emerald murmured, almost to herself. "Does anything even live out there?"

"Quite startling, isn't it? Aside from the marsh spirits—and you can't exactly say they are 'living'—not much can actually survive in Ortland. The evil king lived there, of course. He doesn't have much of a soul. Suppose that's why the marsh spirits didn't bother him. There was also a troll who lived there once. I heard he disappeared. Poor guy. Never really recovered after being banished from Eseland."

"Are you talking about Harry?"

"Yes. Do you know him?"

"No," Emerald said, taking another long look at the desolate landscape miles below their feet. "I met his mother, though."

"Ah, Mavis," the unicorn said. "I heard she was a bit hard on him. She and some of the others in her family. I don't think he ever felt like he fit in with them—or anywhere, really. The name's Bia, by the way."

"Sorry?" asked Emerald. She was lost in her thoughts about how she could empathize with Harry. She didn't feel as though she fit in with her family or anywhere either.

"I'm Bia," the unicorn said again, patiently.

"Oh, I'm, uh, my name is Emerald," Emerald said, flushing with embarrassment. She was glad the unicorn couldn't see her face.

"Nice to meet you, Emerald," Bia said with a slight toss of her head. "We have a little way to go, but I'll have you on the ground soon."

"Um, where are we headed? I was on my way to Eseland."

"Yes, I know. We've been waiting for you. You're our last hope to save Eseland. And that's where I'm taking you."

"Oh," Emerald said, unsure of what else to say. "Um, sorry, but who's we?"

"There's a small group of creatures from Eseland who have been trying to resist the king," Bia responded. "Your godmother is one of them. I am another. There's about a dozen more who haven't been trapped by the king and are trying to find a way to defeat him. Now, rest, child. You'll need your strength where you are going."

Emerald didn't have the energy to argue. The gentle whoosh of the air and the sensation of flying soon lured her to sleep. She didn't wake up again until she felt the thump of them landing on solid ground. She opened her eyes to see that they were now in a clearing in the woods in front of a small cottage. It was a simple wooden building with one window next to the front door. There weren't any flower boxes or gardens to make it look homier, but it didn't feel entirely unwelcoming either.

Emerald slid off the unicorn and looked around. The woods on this side of Ortland didn't look very different from those where she came from. She chuckled a little nervously. "I think I pictured something a bit more . . . magical," Emerald said. Hoping she hadn't offended Bia, she quickly added, "It is very pretty here, though."

Bia's blue-green eyes twinkled. "Yes, it does look rather ordinary right now, doesn't it?" She sighed. "You should see it when it is filled with pixies and imps and every color of butterfly. Then, magical is a perfect way to describe it. So much laughter and color and fun. Hasn't been the same since King Spruce returned." She stamped her front right hoof and snorted. "Well, hopefully you can help us restore our kingdom."

"My godmother thinks I can," Emerald said, uncertainly. She was starting to feel the mounting pressure of her mission. "She's very wise, your godmother," Bia said. She nodded toward the cottage. "You should go in and rest. The tingling from the mist will be gone by morning. Before they disappeared, the border guards used this cottage. I don't think there's much in there, but you should find a bed and blankets. I'll keep watch."

Emerald nodded and started toward the building but turned back. "I don't have much to repay you," Emerald said. The unicorn began to shake her head as if to say don't worry about it. "But I do have food. Would you like something to eat?"

"If all goes well, I'll owe you more than a meal, Princess," Bia said, but she gratefully accepted an apple before nudging Emerald toward the cottage.

Inside it was very simple. The only furniture consisted of a table, two chairs, and a bed with a straw mattress in the corner. There was, however, a fireplace that had plenty of dry kindling in it and a flint next to it to help start the fire. That would be much easier than twisting a stick to make embers. Simple though it was, Emerald was very thankful to spend a night inside. She'd had enough of sleeping under the stars for a while.

Chapter Eighteen

THE EVIL KING

"Head straight down this path, take a right at the river, and continue on until you come to a fork in the road," Bia said to Emerald, giving her directions the next morning before sending the princess on her way. "The king and his daughter are staying in a small house at the end of the path of colored stones."

"Thank you, Bia," Emerald said. She was nervous but energized from her night of rest and a quick breakfast of apples and cheese that morning.

"I would take you myself . . ." Bia said, her voice trailing off a bit sheepishly.

Emerald nodded understandingly. "I know. You can't get close to the king or the stone. Well, wish me luck!"

She hugged the unicorn tightly around the neck, picked up her bow and arrows and flask, and started off down the path. The day was sunny and warm and the forest around her was alive with the sounds of chirping birds. Emerald could almost feel herself relaxing into the comfortable sensation of strolling through the woods on a beautiful day, but a sense of being followed soon whipped that feeling away.

The farther she got from the cottage, the quieter the woods grew. Soon the peaceful day felt threatening and the thick shadows of the trees seemed to close in on her. The sensation that something was watching her, stalking

141

her, only grew stronger as she walked. She looked sharply around multiple times, but nothing disturbed the stillness that had settled into the landscape around her.

The woods were nearly silent by the time she reached the fork in the road Bia described. They were so quiet that the slightest noise made her jump. Though she hadn't seen or heard the sound of any other creature for several hours, she still couldn't shake the feeling that she was being followed. She touched the bow on her back for reassurance.

Emerald regarded her two options as she took a quick swig of water from her flask. One way, guarded by a dense forest of thick, thorny vines led to a beautiful old castle. She could only see the spires of the castle over the vines, but it was like no castle she'd ever seen before. It was large and graceful, like an iced wedding cake, and topped with white marble towers adorned with golden conical roofs shimmering in the sunlight. It was quite a bit more ornate than the sturdy stone castle she lived in.

The other way was the path described by Bia. Colorful stones lined a walkway that led to a cottage. The little house looked as though it had been carved from gingerbread. It had a slanted roof that was just as colorful as the path leading up to the cottage, and the body of the house seemed to be decorated with white icing. Emerald stared at it, remembering stories she'd heard as a child of a witch who lived in such a cottage. The witch had used it to lure in unsuspecting children and make them her dinner.

"Please, sir, you shouldn't be here," said a high-pitched, nervous voice. "Turn back before it's too late."

Emerald shrieked, dropped the flask and spun, peering into the woods behind her. "Show yourself!" she demanded, pulling out her bow, loading it with an arrow, and aiming it in the direction of the voice.

A small wood imp timidly stepped out from the trees. He could have been Maple's brother as much as he looked like her. Emerald gasped and immediately lowered her weapon. She held her hands out, palms up, and crouched down to his level, hoping to show him she was no threat.

"Do you know the king?" she asked, softly. "I was sent here to find him."

The boy shuddered and nodded slowly, but before he could answer they heard a long, slow creak as the door to the cottage began to open. He squeaked before disappearing back into the forest undergrowth.

Emerald's heart pounded loudly as she stared at the opening door. She imagined an ugly, menacing man appearing in the doorway, but to her surprise the man that stepped out was rather handsome and no older than her father. He smiled at Emerald with a mouth full of blindingly white teeth, but she could see an iciness in his pale blue eyes. This must be King Spruce.

"Emerald, Emerald, oh so fair," he purred softly in a voice like fresh butter, "why, oh why, have you come to my lair?"

Emerald was startled that he knew who she was. She drew herself up to her full height, but the stutter in her voice betrayed her nerves.

"I, uh, I've come to ask y—n-n-no tell you to leave our kingdoms alone."

"They sent a child to do a man's work?" the king asked, stroking his chin and grinning mockingly. "How come your father isn't here? Surely the life of a young princess is worth more than that of an old king."

Emerald was about to respond but the king quickly continued before she could get a word in.

"Oh, that's right. The legend. Only a hero of pure intent can defeat me." As he spoke, the king rolled a small, glowing green object around in one hand. His smile grew wider and increasingly more wicked with each word. "Guess your old man is just as corruptible as me."

"He's nothing like you," Emerald retorted, staring at the thing in his hand. That had to be the stone her godmother had told her about. So the rumors were true—the king had somehow gotten the stone back from the troll.

"Beautiful, isn't it?" King Spruce grinned, noticing Emerald's stare. "Don't get any ideas, though. This stone is very precious to me."

Fueled by anger and disgust, Emerald raised her bow again. Maybe she could shoot the stone out of his hands. Before she could draw, though, the king clapped his hands. Her bow and arrow flew out of her hands and landed at King Spruce's feet.

"Now, now," said the king. "A hero of pure intent shouldn't shoot her newest friend, should she? No, that wouldn't do. Let's get to know each other a little better before making any . . . rash decisions, shall we?"

Emerald glared at King Spruce, trying desperately to think of a way to outwit him. He simply held his hand out to her.

"Please, join me. I won't hurt you," he said with his charming coolness. "There are some people I'd like you to meet."

He clapped his hands again and both the wood imp and a sullen young woman of about twenty years old appeared at the king's side.

"This beautiful young woman is my daughter, Raina," the king said proudly, gesturing toward the dour young woman. She had long, wavy blonde hair and blue eyes. She could have been very lovely had it not been for her sour countenance. Raina stared at Emerald moodily.

"Why is she dressed like a boy?" Raina asked snottily,

eyeing Emerald up and down. Emerald suddenly felt self-conscious in her borrowed outfit. Sure, she might have liked something a little prettier, but none of her dresses were really "trooping through the woods and fighting an evil king" appropriate. She made a mental note to design some new adventure clothing for herself—if she made it out of Eseland alive.

"Because she's a hero, darling. I guess that's what heroes are wearing these days."

"Hmmphf," Raina grunted, wrinkling her nose and smoothing the skirt of her own beautiful gown.

"And this"—the king gestured dismissively to the imp—"is Filari. Now, you'll join us for tea," he instructed Emerald. Emerald was about to protest but Filari came up and grabbed her arm. He was stronger than he looked.

"Please be careful with our, ah, guest," the king instructed Filari before turning back to Emerald. "Oh, and I'll be taking your bow and arrows. You won't be needing those here." He snapped his fingers again and the bow and arrows shot up into his hands. He then turned and entered the little house, followed by his daughter.

Filari looked at Emerald apologetically but pushed her forward with a surprising amount of strength. Once inside, the imp shoved Emerald into a wooden chair at a long, knotty table in the middle of the room. He bound her legs but left her hands untied.

"Nice way to treat a guest," Emerald grumbled.

King Spruce, who had taken a seat in another chair at the table, looked up at her and laughed. "Well, we don't want you running off before we've had a chance to talk, do we?" he said. He turned to Filari and snapped his fingers impatiently. "Filari, the tea."

Filari bowed with a frightened look on his face. "Right

away, sir." He darted over to a kettle hanging from a hook on the fireplace.

"So hard to find good help these days," King Spruce complained. "But I suppose you knew that—seeing as you came to face me all alone."

"Er, yes," Emerald responded, looking around the cottage. It was small, but comfortably furnished. It consisted of one big room broken into sleeping, cooking, eating, and sitting areas. Two beds sat against the far wall. A pair of cushioned chairs and a footrest sat close to the stone hearth. She was trying to take note of any and every detail in case something could be used against the evil king.

"Nice place," Emerald said, trying to sound casual. "But why is a powerful king like you living in a cottage?"

"Great question," King Spruce said. "Perhaps you have a few brains in you yet." Emerald tried to keep her face neutral at this remark, but it was really hard. "You see, my dear, when you are king—or queen—half the battle is appearance. I may have some, ahem, power, but how would it look if I just forced my way onto the throne—even if it is rightfully mine? No, my darling daughter here will marry her handsome prince and then no one will be able to question the legitimacy of our claim."

"Won't that make her queen—and her husband, king?" Emerald asked, flicking her eyes at Raina. Raina just stuck out her tongue and continued preening in a small mirror she'd brought to the table. "You'll just be father of the queen."

"Don't worry, my dear, I've thought about that too," King Spruce said, his smile widening. Filari returned to the table carrying a rattling tray topped by a steaming pot of tea and several small porcelain cups. He put a cup in front of the king, Raina, and Emerald with shaking hands and then began serving them. King Spruce paused for a moment to watch

Filari with hawk-like eyes. Though his hands were trembling dangerously, Filari managed to pour the tea without spilling a drop. Once the imp was done, King Spruce picked up his cup and took a sip.

"As I was saying," he continued after swallowing, "I've thought about that too. You're, what, fifteen?"

Emerald nodded suspiciously.

"By my calculations, that makes a princess of Medina ready for engagement," King Spruce said. "Seeing as you are here and not at an engagement celebration, I'm assuming you don't have a fiancé. That means you are eligible to be my wife."

Raina, who'd been quietly sipping her tea in between glances into her mirror, spit her tea into her cup.

"Daddy, no!" she cried. "You can't be serious about marrying this little . . . urchin!"

"Raina, darling"—King Spruce took her hands in his and squeezed them—"I'm giving you the kingdom of Eseland. I have my sights set on something a bit bigger. Medina. And then maybe we'll expand to a few other kingdoms. Together, you and I can rule the entire world." King Spruce smiled fondly at his daughter. She gave him a beautiful smile back.

"Okay, Daddy," Raina dimpled. "But I'm not calling her Mother."

"Of course not, darling," King Spruce conceded. "Filari, where are those scones?"

"Right away, sire." Filari had been frozen by the fireplace watching the exchange between King Spruce and Raina in horror. Now he scrambled to put several scones on a plate and dish up a pot of cream before delivering the food to the table.

Emerald could feel her stomach churning. She couldn't believe she'd run away from an arranged marriage only to be forced into another one—and this one with an evil king who was old enough to be her father!

"What makes you think I'll marry you?" Emerald asked shakily.

"Oh, I don't think I'll have too much trouble convincing you," King Spruce said, taking a bite of scone. He flicked at a few crumbs on his shirt and grinned. "I've put some, shall we say, reassurances in place. I have an army of giants marching toward your kingdom right now. If you don't marry me, they'll crush their way through and take the castle by force."

"How do I know you're telling the truth?" Emerald asked, trying to sound braver than she felt.

"Well, for one, I never lie about something like that," King Spruce said, "but I thought you might say that, so I have another small thing that might convince you. Filari!"

Filari scurried over to a blanket-covered lump in the front corner of the cottage that Emerald had dismissed as a pile of clothes or linens. The imp pulled off the blanket to reveal a young man who was bound hand and foot. His head drooped and he looked seriously ill.

"Porter!" Emerald exclaimed. "What have you done to him?"

"Me?" King Spruce answered innocently. "Why nothing other than take him hostage. We found him and your little imp friend camping near Ortland. She got away somehow, but this one was too sick to move. Seems you've done a good job poisoning him."

"Poisoning him?" Emerald was incredulous. What happened after she left Maple and Porter?

"Yes, poisoning him. Tallyweed doesn't appear to work in humans the way it does in magical creatures. In fact, it looks to have the opposite effect. Your young man is dying. And I'll let him unless . . ."

"Unless?" Emerald asked, though she knew what his demand would be.

"Unless you marry me tomorrow in a double wedding with Raina and her prince." The king smiled at her in an utterly horrible way.

"Daddy! That's my wedding," whined Raina, stamping her foot and pouting.

"It is, darling," King Spruce said soothingly. "We'll just be a small, uh, addendum to your ceremony."

"As long as it's just an ad . . . ad . . ." The spoiled princess frowned faintly as she struggled to get the word out.

"Addendum?" Emerald suggested helpfully.

Raina glared at her. "As long as I'm the star," she huffed. "And my dress has to be prettier."

"Of course, darling." King Spruce put a fond hand on his daughter's face. "You'll be the most beautiful and special bride there ever was."

Pacified, Raina stood up and wandered over to a trunk at the foot of the bed where she pulled out a gorgeous white gown that must be her wedding dress. She held it up to herself and began swaying to some music in her head. King Spruce looked at his daughter with love in his eyes then turned his glance back on Emerald.

"Not thirsty, my darling fiancé?" he asked.

Emerald shuddered. "No, not right now," she responded, looking down at the tea with distaste.

"It's not tallyweed, you know," King Spruce said. "I wouldn't want my future queen getting sick before her big day."

"Of course," Emerald murmured. She stared darkly into her tea. Things were getting out of hand. Get a hold of yourself, Emerald, she thought. Focus on your goal. Get some information about the stone. Be discreet. She was desperate to turn the situation into a positive.

"How did you get the stone back anyway?" Emerald suddenly blurted out, taking the king by surprise. Emerald cringed internally. So much for discreet.

The king regarded Emerald for a long moment and she got the sinking feeling she had lost her chance to learn more about the stone. Finally, however, he cleared his throat and responded.

"Just as they should never send a child to do a man's work, they should also never send a troll to do a witch or wizard's work." He chuckled. "The troll always had a soft spot for my daughter, especially after her mother died. I sent a pigeon to him with a message that Raina was sick—I didn't know if she would pull through. I figured he would do anything to save her, particularly if I told him he was our only hope." He looked off into the distance and murmured, "Sentimental fool."

"So, he came to help you . . . and brought the stone with him?"

"Ah, yes. Harry had to carry it with him wherever he went. It was supposed to prevent the stone from falling into the wrong hands. Raina played her part perfectly. A few rotten berries and some spoiled milk can make almost anyone look like they are on their death bed."

Emerald looked over at Raina who had laid her gown on the bed and was now humming as she brushed her long golden hair. Emerald got the impression that Raina was rather self-absorbed and possibly not that intelligent.

The king went on. "Harry was so distraught to see Raina so desperately ill that he didn't pay attention to me. A quick hit to the head with a log and whoops, little Harry was pretty much dead to the world. I found the stone in his pocket."

"You killed him?" Emerald asked, dread and sadness somersaulting around each other in her stomach.

"No, of course not," the king replied and Emerald sighed in relief. "He may be a fool, but he's a talented fool. I can use his kind of magic. Now, if you'll excuse me"—he pushed away from the table and stood—"I have a few last-minute wedding details to work out. Filari, please tie Emerald's hands back up. I don't need a runaway bride."

Filari came up behind Emerald and pulled her arms behind her back. He wound rope around them tight enough that she couldn't move, but loose enough that they weren't cutting into her skin. The king came over and planted a kiss on the top of Emerald's head, making her almost vomit.

"I'll see you soon, my future wife," he said before turning to Raina. "Darling, Daddy will be back. He's just checking on a few things to make sure your big day is perfect."

Raina lifted a graceful hand in acknowledgment but didn't bother to turn and look at her father. She continued brushing her hair without missing a beat.

Emerald felt like weeping. Porter was dying, her kingdom was in peril, she had no idea where Maple was, and she was going to have to marry the evil king. For someone who was supposed to be a hero, all she'd done so far was mess everything up.

Chapter Nineteen

WEDDING GOWNS AND GIFTS

Emerald was still despairing a few hours later when the king returned from whatever he'd been doing.

"Oh, darling," he said to Emerald upon reentering the cottage, "I've invited your parents to our wedding. I figured they'd be proud to know their daughter had picked a husband and was so eager to marry him she wasn't going to wait any longer."

Emerald felt even worse, if that were possible. She was sure this was a trap for her parents. After all, King Spruce couldn't rule Medina with her parents still alive.

The king ordered Filari to prepare a hasty dinner before ordering everyone to bed.

"Tomorrow is a big day," he grinned. "Both of you brides need your beauty sleep." Raina smiled prettily at this and Emerald turned pale. "Good night, my darlings," King Spruce said.

Filari helped Emerald to a pile of old potato sacks on the floor on which to sleep. He kept her hands and feet bound, though. Emerald lay down but wasn't the least bit sleepy. Once she could hear soft snores coming from the king, she shifted herself to get a better look around the cabin. As she did, her eyes settled on the little imp who was curled up in the corner across from her, watching her with big dark eyes.

"Filari," she whispered. He shot a frightened look toward the king before looking back to Emerald. "Come here, I won't hurt you."

Filari crept slowly and carefully toward her until he was next to her. He kept glancing fearfully over his shoulder at the sleeping king.

"You've got to help me escape. I'm here to help you—to save the kingdom," Emerald whispered.

Filari shook his little head vigorously. "Filari can't, Princess. The master, he cursed Filari. If Filari defies him, Filari will grow a wart."

"Grow a wart?" Emerald wondered how that, other than not looking great, could be all that bad.

"Yes, Filari will grow a wart and then the master will know Filari betrayed him. He'll punish Filari severely if he betrays the master." He shuddered.

"But you tried to warn me—" Emerald started.

"Shhh," he hissed. "Filari will pay for that, he will. Filari is scared, Princess. Scared and a coward."

"You are no coward, Filari. I'll prove it to you." Emerald considered him carefully. "The king didn't order you not to talk to me, right?"

Filari shook his head, then nodded, then shook his head again in confusion as he tried to figure out the right answer.

"Well, then maybe you can tell me a bit more about him and Raina," Emerald suggested. He nodded again slowly, but his eyes were still dark with fear.

"Let's start with something easy. Tell me about the prince who is supposed to marry Raina," Emerald began. "What did the king do to him and his family?"

"It was very bad, Princess." He swallowed hard. "The master turned the king and queen into stone and put the prince under a spell."

"Why hasn't the wedding happened yet?" Surely the king hadn't been waiting for Emerald's arrival to marry his daughter to the prince.

"Raina isn't so smart, but she's very vain," Filari said, looking a bit guilty. "She wants the biggest, most glamorous wedding ever seen. Everyone in Eseland has been pulled into working around the clock to get things ready."

"And the king bends to her will that easily?" Emerald asked, though she already had a sneaking suspicion that Raina might be his weakness.

"Yes. She's the only daughter of the master's one true love. The master may be evil, but he really loved Raina's mother. The master's never forgiven himself for her death."

"So, Raina is all he has left of her," Emerald said, more to herself than to Filari.

"Yes. The master would do anything for her. I think she's the only one who has power over the master—not that he would admit it," Filari said. He was sweating and kept turning his hands and arms this way and that, peering at them. "Do you, er, see any warts on Filari?"

Emerald looked the imp over, but in the dim light of the moon shining through the cracks in the shutters on the window she didn't see anything.

"No," she reassured him. "It looks like you are fine. Now go back to sleep. I won't ask you any more."

The little imp gratefully scampered back to his corner and turned his back to Emerald after settling down.

Emerald had to come up with a plan to stop the evil king, and it sounded like her solution lay in his spoiled daughter. She looked over at Porter who was still unconscious in his bindings on the floor. Fortunately, she could still see the rise and fall of his chest in the moonlight. She hoped she had enough time to save him.

As dawn broke the next morning, Emerald was still pondering how she could exploit King Spruce's love for his daughter in order to defeat him. When the first golden rays of the sun began to creep through the shutters, King Spruce stretched and rolled out of bed. Emerald pretended to be sleeping as he rose and shot a sharp glance at his captives, but she kept her eyes open just a crack to see what he would do.

King Spruce stood over his sleeping daughter's bed for a moment and tenderly brushed a strand of hair from her face. Raina was actually rather pretty. She had the golden hair of the princesses in the stories Emerald read as a child. Her skin was smooth and her cheekbones high. Her mother must have been very beautiful.

Breaking his gentle moment over his daughter, the king turned and strode over to where Filari was sleeping on the floor. He towered above the imp and cleared his throat sharply. Startled, Filari's eyes flew open and he snapped to attention, jumping quickly to his feet.

"Breakfast," demanded the king. "And make sure my daughter has hot water for a bath."

The little imp bowed and scrambled quickly to the fireplace where he began to rouse the fire from its banked state.

"Wait," the king said sharply, peering closely at the back of Filari's neck. "What is that?"

Filari's hand flew to the back of his neck and his eyes grew wide. There was a wart, and not just a normal wart. This was big and bulbous—it could be seen from across the room where Emerald lay.

"You betrayed me, didn't you, you filthy little creature. What did you do?" The king pointed his wand at the little imp who was shaking like a leaf and backing slowly into the corner.

"F-F-F-ilari d-d-d-oesn't k-k-k-now!" Filari stuttered weakly. The king raised his wand high over his head.

"Wait!" yelled Emerald, doing her best to push herself into

a seated position. It was very difficult being bound hand and foot, and she was only able to shift herself into an awkward, leaning pose. "It's probably my fault."

The king turned and regarded Emerald skeptically.

"Oh yes? How so?"

"Well, last night after you went to bed I asked Filari for a bit of scone." Emerald was quite impressed that she was able to come up with a lie so easily. "I was hungry. He didn't want to, but I said I'd scream and wake you up. That you'd be even madder about that than if he just let me eat. So, he brought me some scone . . ." Emerald trailed off, hoping the king didn't know how many scones should have been left after yesterday's tea.

"Is that so?" The king turned to the imp. Filari nodded weakly. The king didn't look convinced, but he dropped his wand. "Very well. I'll let it go this time," he said generously.

"I can't have my bride fainting from hunger on her wedding day." He turned and added sharply to Filari, "But if I ever find out you have betrayed me, I'll make that wart grow until it consumes your entire body. Now get breakfast ready."

Filari quickly bent over his work preparing the morning meal. The king, meanwhile, walked over to Emerald and lifted her into the seated position she had been trying to achieve.

"Sleep well, my beauty?" he asked coyly. "It's our big day. What say I untie your arms and legs, eh? You won't run away now, will you?" The king looked pointedly at Porter as he said the last sentence.

Emerald shook her head but let King Spruce help her to her feet. "You sure know how to woo a woman," Emerald muttered sulkily, trying to sound like a defeated prisoner.

The king's smile only grew in delight of her misery. "I didn't peg you as the romantic type. Still, if it's romance you desire . . ."

The king put his hand behind his back and brought it back out again with a bouquet of blood-red roses, which he presented to Emerald with a flourish. She eyed them suspiciously.

"Go on, take them," he insisted. "They won't bite!"

Emerald hesitantly took the bouquet from his hands. As the stems touched her fingers, the flowers shriveled up and turned into dust, crumbling onto the floor. The king laughed at the shocked look on her face.

"Filari, get over here and clean up this mess," he barked, still laughing. He lifted Emerald's chin and stared into her eyes coldly. "I don't have to romance you to make you mine."

Emerald shivered as he walked away. She had to come up with a plan—and fast. There was no way she was going to marry this malevolent man.

Roused by the noises being made or the smell of bread baking on the fire, Raina slowly stirred and got out of bed herself. She stretched lazily then suddenly jumped excitedly to her feet.

"It's my wedding day!" she exclaimed.

Her father hurried to her side and embraced her, saying, "That it is, my princess, that it is."

"Daddy, it is going to be the biggest, most beautiful wedding anyone's ever seen, right?" She looked up at her father with big, expectant eyes.

The king smiled and nodded. "Yes, my darling. It will be a wedding that is talked about for centuries to come," he promised. "Now why don't you eat something and get ready. We have a wedding to attend!"

Raina hugged her father and squealed excitedly. She then hurried to the table where Filari deposited a couple of bowls of oatmeal and two steaming cups of tea.

"Filari, I'll take my breakfast outside so the brides can get ready," King Spruce instructed. "Fill the tub with hot water and then bring Porter and the food outside." He then walked over to the trunk at the foot of the bed and pulled out a simple but pretty white dress. "This is for you," he said, turning to Emerald.

Raina looked at the dress suspiciously, but apparently satisfied that it couldn't compete with her own extravagant gown, turned back to her oatmeal. He brought the dress to Emerald who took it cautiously, expecting it to crumble or turn into something else after the king's little stunt with the flowers.

"Don't worry, this isn't a trick," King Spruce said. "I want my bride to look like a bride on her big day. Now eat and get ready."

With that, he left the cottage. Filari quickly poured hot water from the kettle on the stove into a small silver tub sitting near the fireplace. He grabbed a third bowl of oatmeal and took that outside before returning to drag a barely conscious Porter out the door. Porter's clouded eyes briefly met Emerald's on the way out, but she couldn't tell if he actually recognized her.

The two princesses ate their breakfast in silence. Emerald was very hungry by now and figured she could use a big meal to help keep her on her toes today. If she was going to win Raina to her side, now was the time to do it. After they finished their meal, Emerald offered to help Raina get ready. The princess looked suspicious but accepted Emerald's offer. She wanted a little pampering on her wedding day.

"Have you met the prince?" Emerald asked, picking up Raina's brush and running it through Raina's thick locks as the spoiled princess bathed.

"Oh yes," cooed Raina. "He is very handsome. The handsomest prince in the land. That is why I have to be the most beautiful bride ever. He's going to fall in love with me and I'm going to be queen and we are going to live happily ever after."

"He is very lucky, that's for sure," Emerald said as sincerely as she could. It apparently wasn't very convincing, though, because Raina shot her a sharp look.

"Are you making fun of me?"

Emerald shook her head and tried harder. "No, I just . . . you are just very beautiful. That's all." Truthfully, she added, "You have the prettiest hair I've ever seen."

"Yes." Raina nodded in agreement. "You're right. I'm sure it must be hard to be stuck with hair like yours. I suppose it would be hard to get any prince to love you."

Emerald hung her head as if in shame, though she was really trying to keep from laughing. She kept picturing all the princes who had tried to win her hand and heart.

"I saw that beautiful stone your father has. Is that your wedding present?" Emerald inquired cautiously.

Raina shook her head. "No, that's Daddy's favorite stone. It reminds him of my mother. My real mother."

"Oh," said Emerald sheepishly, handing Raina a towel as she stepped out of the tub. "It's just so beautiful, I thought it would look stunning in a necklace for your wedding day."

Raina dried off and put on her undergarments. She let Emerald help her into her long white gown, which was covered in tiny diamonds and pearls. Emerald thought Raina must have just brushed off her statement about the stone, but she turned to her mirror and touched her bare neck thoughtfully.

"You're right," she said finally. "It should be mine."

Emerald nodded encouragingly but said nothing more about the necklace. Instead she turned to benign talk about the wedding decorations and details. She hoped she had planted a seed that would work.

A short while later, the king reentered the cottage to collect his daughter and bride for the wedding.

"Are you decent?" he said after knocking and cracking the door open.

"Yes, come in, Daddy!" Raina said, posing to give the king the best possible view of her dress when he walked in. King Spruce's eyes shone with what Emerald thought might be tears as he looked at his daughter in her wedding gown.

"Oh, Raina," he said mistily. "You look beautiful. So much like your mother."

Raina smiled. "Speaking of Mommy—Daddy, I want my wedding present."

The king looked confused. "What? I mean, of course! After your wedding, I will give you your choice of castles and villages to rule. I'm not sure what that has to do with Mommy, but I'll—"

"No, Daddy. I want my present now. I want your green stone. I want it in a necklace."

The king shot a dark look at Emerald before responding to his daughter. "Darling, you know I would give you anything, but I can't give you that stone."

"I. Want. IT!" screamed Raina, stomping her feet. She began to pull at her hair and dress while the king stared at her helplessly. He alternated between glaring at Emerald and trying feebly to calm his daughter. Emerald was amazed at the power the girl had over her father.

At that moment, Filari came back into the cottage dragging a zombie-like Porter. He stared with horror at the sight of Raina stamping and screaming, the king looking flustered, and Emerald trying to look as blank as possible.

"Did you have something to do with this?" the king growled at Emerald. She shook her head, but he angrily stormed over to Porter. He grabbed the young man by his arm and yanked him over to the fireplace. Once there, he pulled a handful of green leaves from a box on top of the mantel. "Perhaps we should give him one more dose of this. He'll probably not make it through that, of course . . ."

Emerald shook her head frantically and cried, "No! I'll do anything. Please just leave him alone."

"Kindly convince my daughter that she doesn't need my stone," the king said through gritted teeth as he held the tallyweed dangerously close to Porter's mouth.

"Okay, okay, just please don't hurt him," Emerald sobbed, trying to think of how to calm the princess. Her plan had backfired, badly. Remembering back to her cousin's wedding and what had made her cousin nervous, she made an attempt at soothing Raina.

"You know, Raina," she began shakily, "I've actually heard that green is a bad luck color on wedding days. So maybe your father's stone isn't the best thing to wear today. You need a . . . a pearl necklace! Yes, something as pure and beautiful as you."

Raina stopped stomping and screaming, but she still looked unconvinced. The king quickly jumped in to back up Emerald's statement.

"She's right," he declared. "Maybe we can talk about the stone after your wedding, but today you should wear white." He pulled his wand from his pocket and waved it, making a beautiful strand of pearls appear. He dropped his grip on Porter, who slumped to the floor, and held out the pearls to his daughter. Distracted by the beautiful necklace, Raina let her father fasten it around her neck and then preened into the mirror, lightly touching it with her fingers.

"Perfect," she declared.

"Yes, you are," her father agreed.

Emerald groaned internally. It looked like she was getting married today.

Chapter Twenty

A Royal Double Wedding

Emerald had never been so scared and sad in her life. Why hadn't she listened to everyone who told her that she shouldn't try to fight or be a hero? Sure, Queen Ellyn had been able to defeat a dragon and protect her people, but Emerald wasn't Queen Ellyn. She obviously wasn't that strong and she certainly wasn't feeling very brave. At this point she felt like she had ruined everything. Porter was sick and a prisoner, her kingdom was going to be controlled by evil King Spruce, and the life of every magical creature—and perhaps every human too—was in danger. She could practically hear her mother say, "I told you so."

"Ladies first." King Spruce held out his hands to his daughter and Emerald to help them into a carriage that would take them to the castle for the double wedding. The king had enchanted the carriage to shine as if it were covered by millions of tiny diamonds. He noticed Emerald eyeing it disdainfully. He leaned toward her. "Image is everything, my dear. We want everyone in Eseland to see and respect our power." He chortled evilly. "Not that they have a choice, of course."

"Of course," murmured Emerald. She accepted his helping hand up into the carriage and slid next to her soon-to-be stepdaughter on a heavily cushioned bench. Everything was so ridiculous. Here she was riding in an enchanted carriage that, as far as she could tell, no one would see but their little wedding party, and she was about to become wife to a man old enough to be her father, thus making her stepmother to a woman older than she.

"Oh, cheer up," said Raina. "It's our wedding day!" She then added as an afterthought, "You even look kind of pretty. Better than you did in those boy clothes anyway."

"Thanks," Emerald responded dryly. She was wearing a modest white gown that was fitted to the waist then flared out gracefully. A modest golden belt hung from her waist and gauzy sleeves covered her arms to her wrists. Raina had simply but elegantly pulled Emerald's hair back with a couple of combs. Emerald had been forbidden from wearing her leather pouch, but she was now wearing a plain golden necklace that King Spruce gave her as a "wedding present." Raina's dress, meanwhile, was quite ostentatious, with its poufy sleeves, billowy skirts and glittering diamond embellishments. She wore a tiara of diamonds, pearls, and gold in her silken hair which hung to her waist. Even if it wasn't a forced marriage, Emerald could imagine the prince of Eseland falling in love with the beautiful girl at first sight.

Emerald was startled from her thoughts as King Spruce shoved Porter, still bound and gagged, roughly into the carriage. He was actually starting to look a little better. There was some color in his cheeks and his eyes looked sharper as he met Emerald's eyes.

"A little insurance, my dear, to make sure you don't forget your vows," King Spruce said to Emerald, noticing the look she shared with Porter. "Now that we are all here, let's go have a wedding!" He snapped his fingers and shouted out the window, "Coachman—to the castle!"

The carriage made its way down the colorful path and turned onto the main road leading to the castle. As they approached the thick forest of vines, the tangled plants magically bowed out of the way to reveal a road. The horses sped down the road and the vines closed back together behind them. Emerald felt as if she were being swallowed whole by the jaws of a great monster.

"So, my dear Emerald, after we are married, we will take a little honeymoon to Medina," King Spruce said, leaning forward and putting a hand on Emerald's knee. She jerked at his touch, which made him chuckle wickedly. "I'm sure everyone will want to meet your new husband and celebrate their new king and queen."

"You won't be king," Emerald spat back, brushing the king's hand away. "My father is still alive."

"Minor detail," King Spruce responded, removing his hand from her knee and waving it dismissively. Emerald felt a chill run down her spine. "He'll give up his throne if he knows what's good for him. Otherwise . . ." King Spruce shrugged, but Emerald didn't need him to finish his thought to understand his meaning. She stared hard at the floor, willing herself not to cry. Porter shifted in his seat a bit, but Emerald didn't dare look at him. She was sure her will would break if she did.

"Daddy, look! They're all here to see me!" Raina, oblivious to her father's and Emerald's conversation, pointed out the window excitedly. Emerald looked where she was pointing and, to her surprise, the vines were now gone and a crowd of magical creatures lined both sides of the road, waving and cheering. Despite her predicament, Emerald was transfixed. She could hardly believe her eyes to see so many incredible beings of which she'd only dreamed. There were stoic centaurs, delicate fairies, exquisite elves, enchanting nymphs, tiny pixies, and even fearsome harpies. Little wrinkled gnomes stood side-by-side with towering ogres, while colorfully dressed witches and wizards jumped up and down like small children on their birthdays. As awe-inspiring as the creatures were, Emerald thought there was also something very odd about them. She stared harder and realized that they all had very glassy eyes. It was like staring at a crowd of sleepwalkers.

This fact went unnoticed by Raina, who waved back and blew kisses. The crowds continued even after the carriage drove over the castle drawbridge and into the courtyard. Once the carriage stopped, Filari jumped down from his spot next to the driver and opened the door. He bowed to King Spruce, Emerald, and Raina as they stepped out.

"Take this one to the throne room, and make sure she'll be able to see him," King Spruce demanded, gesturing first to Porter and then to Emerald.

"Yes, Your Majesty." Filari clapped his hands and two guards appeared and dragged Porter from the carriage and up to the castle. King Spruce, meanwhile, took a few moments to smile and wave at the glassy-eyed crowd. Up close, the zombie-like state of the enchanted creatures was even spookier, but that didn't seem to bother the king or his daughter.

King Spruce offered an arm each to his daughter and Emerald and escorted them up the flawless white marble staircase to the entrance of the castle. Emerald stumbled a little as they neared the top.

"Don't worry, my dear," King Spruce murmured to her as he steadied her, "everyone is nervous on their wedding day." Emerald looked at him dubiously. "Well, not me, of course," he added. "I just feel powerful. There was another time, though . . ." His voice trailed off and he got a distant look in his eyes. Emerald wondered if he was thinking about Raina's mother. The moment didn't last long, though. King Spruce shook his head and drove them forward as the elaborately carved wooden doors swung open to admit them.

They entered a foyer with bright white marble floors and

even whiter walls. Just as many spectators were inside as there were outside. Elaborate arrangements of flowers adorned every nook and cranny; sprays of pink roses and white ranunculus spilled out of tall, freestanding golden vases while garlands of the same flowers were hung from windows and walls. Beautiful crystal chandeliers cast sparkling rainbows of light on the walls, floors, and guests. Though a bit ostentatious, Emerald had to admit that it was also beautiful.

"Do you like it, my darling?" King Spruce asked Raina. She was staring around the room with wide eyes and an open mouth.

"Oh, yes, Daddy," she breathed happily. "It's even more wonderful than I imagined."

They crossed the foyer and neared the throne room doors, which were still closed. King Spruce let go of Emerald's arm and turned to Filari, who'd turned back up after taking care of Porter.

"When these doors open, I'll escort Raina down the aisle. You follow with Emerald. Don't start until we are halfway down"—he pinned Filari with a glare—" because Raina deserves to have all eyes on her today."

From inside the throne room, Emerald could hear the music swelling. She flashed back to about a week earlier when she stood in front of another pair of doors, waiting for her life to change. That seemed an eternity ago.

Suddenly the doors opened and the crowds inside turned back to see the brides enter the room. They all had looks of admiration plastered on their faces. King Spruce smiled at the guests before shooting a quick, cold glance back at Filari and Emerald.

"No funny business," he said icily and then turned back to walk his daughter down the aisle. Emerald watched their backs, racking her brain for ideas to stop the wedding.

Without the stone, there wasn't much hope. Emerald looked down at Filari. Maybe he . . .? But no, the little imp looked up at her with frightened eyes and then quickly turned forward again. Sighing, Emerald stepped forward with Filari and began walking down the aisle.

As they neared the end of the aisle, Emerald stole a glance at the prince Raina was going to marry. He was a handsome young elf, tall and blond. He had a grin plastered on his face, but his green eyes looked completely blank.

"Who gives this woman to wed this man?" the officiant asked robotically as Raina and her father reached the steps at the base of the throne. Clearly, he was enchanted as well.

"I do," the king responded proudly. Emerald stepped next to Raina and looked at the king. She could swear she saw tears glistening in his eyes and had to bite down on her tongue to keep from laughing. You'd think Raina and the king were participants in a real wedding rather than the masterminds behind an enchanted one, she thought snidely. A quick glance past the king, though, sobered her up. Porter was still bound hand and foot and being held between two guards who had swords pointed at his throat.

"And who gives this woman to wed . . ." A faint frown creased the officiant's brow as he looked at Emerald.

"Me. She's marrying me," King Spruce responded authoritatively. "And he gives her." He pointed at Filari.

"Yes, of course," the officiant said, though it was obvious nothing was really registering to him.

"Raina first. The traditional ceremony," commanded the king. "Then you can marry Emerald and me. The short version is fine." He turned to Emerald and asked in a sickly-sweet voice, "That okay with you, my dear?"

Unable to speak, Emerald's eyes darted quickly to Porter. The guards gripped him a little tighter and she could see him wince as the points of their swords pricked into his neck. Emerald swallowed and simply nodded in response. Satisfied, the king turned his focus back to his daughter and the enchanted prince.

"Dearly beloved, we are gathered here today . . ." As the officiant droned on, Emerald stole a quick glance around her to see if anyone was at least halfway conscious. There had to be someone who could help her. She didn't think there was much hope, though, if she couldn't get the stone from the king.

Sighing, Emerald rubbed her hands together. As she did, her fingers ran over something sharp and cold. Her godmother's ring! In all the confusion and fear of Porter's capture, she'd forgotten all about it. Emerald rubbed her fingers over the pink stone and felt her mind running through all the people she knew who might be able to hear her silent plea for assistance. Suddenly her great-grandmother came to mind. Oh, Queen Ellyn, Emerald begged, please come to your great-granddaughter's assistance! Emerald felt all her inner being focus on her cry to her great-grandmother. It was as if something powerful was swirling up inside her and reaching a hand out to the heavens.

Suddenly the light streaming through the large windows at the front of the throne room went dark, as though a big storm cloud had moved in front of the sun. Emerald stared and saw the glass vibrate from some powerful force outside. It vibrated harder and harder then shattered, sending sparkling shards in every direction.

Emerald grabbed Filari, who was standing next to her, and dove away from the steps. She made her move just in time because in the next instant a huge, green, clawed foot came crashing down in the very spot where they had been standing. Emerald looked over and saw that the king had pulled Raina out of the way as well. The glassy-eyed prince now stood unflinchingly between two enormous scaly feet. Emerald stared at them and then slowly raised her eyes up the rest of the creature's body. Four powerful legs connected with a muscular body topped by a long neck and big head. The head featured a long snout that was slightly open and puffing small clouds of smoke. Red eyes, razor-sharp teeth, and impressive wings completed the creature's appearance. Emerald gasped. It was a dragon.

Emerald didn't know what was scarier—the dragon or the fact that the entire room was silent. The crowd of enchanted onlookers was not even fazed by the dragon. They just stared in their eerily blank way.

Emerald felt frozen herself, unsure what to do next. Was this the help she had asked for? King Spruce wasn't so hesitant. He rose to his feet and held up his stone, talking slowly and in a low voice to the menacing beast.

"Hello, my beauty. Let's be friends, shall we?" he said, putting his body between the dragon and his daughter. The dragon stared down at the king ferociously but followed the stone with his blood-red eyes.

"Move, you fool," King Spruce hissed at the prince who stumbled away from the dragon. Fortunately for the prince, the dragon kept his eyes on the stone.

Emerald noticed Raina creeping farther and farther back down the aisle. This was Emerald's chance. If she was going to do anything, it had to be now while King Spruce was distracted. She looked around the floor and found a large shard of glass. Grabbing it, she bounded over to Raina and seized her, holding the glass to Raina's throat. Raina screamed.

Both the dragon and King Spruce whirled around at the commotion. The king's eyes widened in shock.

"Just what do you think you are doing?" he hissed furiously.

"Forcing you to make a choice—the stone or your daughter," Emerald responded, her voice sounding much more confident than she felt. "Throw it to me. I'll take care of the dragon and you can have your daughter back."

"Foolish child," sneered the king. "You don't even know how to use the stone."

The dragon snarled and took a step toward Emerald and Raina. King Spruce quickly turned back to it and raised the stone again.

"There, there, my pretty. We'll find you something to eat, hmm?" King Spruce cooed. "How about that stable boy over there?" He gestured toward Porter and the dragon's head swung to look where the king was pointing. A slimy string of saliva slowly trailed from its mouth.

"Guards, bring him here!" King Spruce ordered and the guards dragged Porter toward the dragon. Emerald gasped and tightened her grip on Raina. Raina was trembling in Emerald's arms but had been quiet since her initial scream. She emitted a little gasp and Emerald looked down, noticing in horror a small drop of blood where she'd accidentally pressed the shard of glass too hard.

"Sorry," whispered Emerald. Raina looked up at Emerald with frightened eyes but didn't say anything.

Porter was now at the dragon's feet and the dragon was eyeing him hungrily. King Spruce still held the stone above his head, though, so the dragon did nothing more than salivate over his soon-to-be dinner.

"Now, my dear, it appears you have a choice to make," King Spruce said evenly. "Your young friend here in exchange for my daughter. A life for a life."

Emerald looked back and forth between the king and Porter, rattled. She hadn't anticipated King Spruce calling her bluff when it came to the life of his daughter. She figured he would do anything he could to save Raina. She stole a glance down at the princess who looked pale and terrified. Raina stared pleadingly at Emerald but was too terrified to speak.   Emerald forced down her feelings of pity for the king's daughter and looked back at Porter who shook his head weakly. He didn't want Emerald to give up her advantage. The dragon shuffled his giant feet and began huffing out puffs of smoke. She didn't have much time, but the rush of emotion that swept through Emerald caused her to hesitate. As bad as she felt for Raina, she was devastated at the thought of losing Porter. He'd done nothing but try to help her all of her life. In return, all she'd done was put him in some pretty terrible situations. She racked her brain desperately to think of any other way to end the stalemate and still come out ahead, but she couldn't risk appearing weak and losing her only leverage.

Emerald felt as though she was peeling her soul from her body. It didn't feel heroic to sacrifice one of her best friends, but she couldn't see that she had any other choice.

"I'm sorry," Emerald mouthed to Porter, who tried to smile, though the fear in his eyes betrayed him. She looked back at King Spruce and stared steadily into his eyes. It was her turn to call the king's bluff. "No deal," she said with deadly calm. King Spruce looked shocked. He hadn't anticipated Emerald's boldness and was clearly more than a bit flustered as he turned back to the dragon and said, "Eat him."

The dragon opened its mouth and a ball of fire began to form at the back of its throat. The entire room filled with the smell of sulfur. Porter squeezed his eyes shut, but Emerald wouldn't let herself look away. She made a choice and now she had to face it. Even worse, she was going to have to follow through with her threat to Raina. Tears ran down her face as she silently said goodbye to one of her best friends and tightened her grip on Raina. The princess whimpered.

Emerald cringed at the thought of hurting her, but she knew she needed to steel her resolve.

"Emerald!"

A voice shook Emerald out of her horrified trance. She looked down to her right and saw a familiar face poking out between the legs of a centaur. Maple!

"What are you doing here?" Emerald hissed.

"Bia brought me. I thought you might want this." Maple grinned, holding out Queen Ellyn's bow and quiver of arrows. "Boy, this sure is a dull wedding. But you look gorgeous! Here, catch! I'll take her."

Maple threw the bow and quiver to Emerald and scurried over to take the glass and hold it to Raina's throat. Even though Maple was much smaller than Raina, the princess was too frightened to struggle.

Emerald looked up just in time to see the ball of fire grow brighter and the dragon's mouth dip over Porter's head. King Spruce was laughing evilly, still holding the stone high in the air. She took aim and loosed the string. Her arrow flew across the room and struck the dragon right in the middle of one of its red eyes.

"Bullseye!" Emerald whispered, feeling a rush of adrenaline from her perfect shot.

The dragon roared in pain and threw its head to the sky. Fire emitted from deep in its belly, searing the white ceiling black. Porter opened his eyes and looked up at the dragon, trembling. He threw himself down the steps and rolled away as King Spruce spun around to face Emerald. The king's face was white with fury.

"How dare you!" he sputtered, his blazing eyes coming to rest on Emerald. "You'll regret that."

"Not as much as you will," Emerald responded coolly. She loosed a second arrow, striking the king in his hand

and making him drop the stone. He screamed in pain and grabbed his hand, the arrow sticking through it. In the midst of the confusion, Filari scrambled across the floor, grabbed the stone, and darted back to where he started. He stared at the stone, entranced.

"Filari, give that back to me," snarled King Spruce. "If you don't, I promise you'll pay."

Filari looked back at the king, clearly frightened and unsure what to do.

"That's right, give it back," King Spruce said encouragingly. "You've always been such a big help to me."

Filari took a step towards the king. King Spruce smiled and nodded at the imp. Filari was about to take another step but stopped suddenly. His eyes widened as he watched the dragon open its jaw and drop its head. Before King Spruce could even react, the dragon swallowed him up in one bite. Emerald, Filari, Maple, Porter, and Raina stared in disbelief, but the rest of the creatures in the room began to applaud quietly, as if cheering at the kiss of a newly married couple.

Filari was the first to come out of shock. He shouted, "Emerald—catch!" and threw the stone to the surprised princess. Instinct made her drop her bow to throw her hands up and catch the stone. Once in her hands, it felt strangely warm and seemed to pulse.

The dragon swung its head toward Emerald and lurched forward. It was clearly furious about the arrow in its eye. Emerald whirled and ran. The king was right—she didn't know how to use the stone and she didn't have time to learn. "Emerald, duck!" she heard Maple cry. She hit the floor just in time to see a burst of flames above her head. Emerald heard a shriek of pain from her friend but didn't dare take the time to turn and see if she was all right. She scrambled to her feet and began running again.

"Emerald, watch out!" Filari squealed. Emerald dove sharply to her left, hoping she picked the right direction. Fortunately, she had and she felt the heat of another burst of flames that narrowly missed her to the right. She heard cries of agony from some bystanders who weren't so lucky.

Emerald stood to run again but quickly found herself blocked by the closed doors at the rear of the throne room. She spun around and stared up in terror. The giant, fire-breathing creature stalked closer and closer, like a cat ready to pounce on its prey. It opened its mouth, drooling. Emerald could smell the sulfuric smoke from the dragon's acrid breath. She was trapped!

A giant ball of fire formed at the back of the dragon's throat. Emerald could feel the heat of the flames even before they erupted from the dragon's mouth. Not knowing what else to do, she flung the stone toward the back of its throat. She then hit the floor and curled into a tight ball as the flames engulfed her.

There was a loud bang. Then silence and darkness.

Chapter Twenty-One

As the Dust Settles

Smothering darkness and a ringing in her ears. That was all Emerald could sense as her eyes fluttered open. She felt numb from head to feet. Why was everything so dark? Had she been killed by the dragon's flames? She tried wriggling her fingers and toes. Good, she could still feel them. Slowly, her mind began to clear and sensation began working its way back into her limbs. The ringing in her ears started to die away and was replaced by the sounds of shouts, crying, and pounding feet. She could also hear someone calling her name.

"Emerald! Emerald! Are you okay? Emerald?"

Emerald pushed herself up and felt some kind of heavy material fall from her shoulders. She stared down at it. It was her godmother's favorite robin's egg–blue cloak. Apparently, it was not only pretty—it was dragon fire–proof. It didn't have a burn on it. But wait, if she had her godmother's cloak, that could only mean—

"Godmother!" Emerald said, her mind finally clearing enough to make sense of what was going on. She rubbed her bleary eyes and looked up to meet her godmother's concerned violet eyes.

"Oh, thank goodness," Elyria said, relief heavy in her voice. "I was afraid I wouldn't be in time."

"You saved me!" Emerald cried, throwing her arms around her godmother, who looked a little more disheveled than normal. Her curly white hair was sticking out in various

176

directions and she had smudges of soot on her face and hands. Still, she looked unscathed.

"And you saved them," her godmother responded, pushing Emerald back after a moment to gesture toward the confused mass of fairytale creatures around them. Some were crying and hugging, others were staring around in confusion. A couple of centaurs were trying to organize help for the injured. The body of the dragon lay unmoving in the middle of the room and a shimmering green haze hovered in the air.

"The stone?" Emerald asked, still trying to make sense of what happened.

"It exploded when you threw it into the dragon's mouth," Elyria explained. "It was strong enough to stand up against magic, but apparently not strong enough to withstand dragon fire. The dragon didn't make it either."

"The people of Eseland? They're all back to normal?" Emerald looked around at fairies, elves, pixies, centaurs, imps, and nymphs who, though shocked, seemed to be fully functional again.

"Yes, thanks to you. Once the stone was gone, the spell was broken," Elyria said.

"What about you? I mean, I have your cloak." Emerald held out the cloak with a worried look on her face.

"Fortunately, my wand has better aim than my arm," Elyria said, winking. "Bia brought me through the open window after she left Maple on the castle stairs. Bless that unicorn—she does fly fast. We flew in just as you threw the stone in the dragon's mouth. A quick flick of my wand and, poof, you were covered by my cloak."

"Thank you," Emerald said, gratefully. Suddenly she remembered something else. "Maple! Porter! Filari!" Where were her friends? She tried pushing herself to her feet but found she was a bit unsteady. Her godmother put her arms around Emerald and helped her up.

"Let's find them," her godmother said.

They pushed their way through the crowd toward the front of the throne room, Emerald still holding on to Elyria a bit for support. As they did, many of the creatures bowed reverently out of Emerald's way. Some even touched her gently on the arms and whispered, "Thank you." Emerald tried to smile and nod back, but she was too worried about her friends to focus on much else.

When they neared the stairs, they found Raina huddled over a small form. Her slender shoulders were shaking as she sobbed. Porter was next to her, thankfully untied and looking the best he had in days. He was on his knees and stroking the head of whomever lay in Raina's arms. Filari stood with his hand on Raina's shoulder. He looked up, meeting Emerald's eyes with a mournful expression.

"Maple," whispered Emerald, dashing over to the little group. Raina looked up as Emerald reached her and Emerald could see the limp body of the little imp in her arms.

"She saved me," Raina whispered hoarsely, tears streaming down her face. Her blonde hair hung in tangled strands around her head and her pretty white dress was torn and dirty. Surprisingly, Raina didn't seem to notice or care.

"Maple! Maple, wake up!" Emerald cried, sinking to her knees next to Raina and grabbing Maple's cold hand.

"What happened?" Elyria asked Raina.

"The dragon, it . . . it nearly stepped on us. Maple, she pushed me." Raina's voice cracked as she spoke. "She pushed me away. He got her though."

Emerald's godmother put her hands gently on the little imp's body and shook her head softly. "Crushed," she murmured. "He missed her chest and head, thankfully, but her legs . . ." Elyria's voice trailed off and a look of utter sorrow filled her eyes.

"Wait—you have powers!" Emerald said frantically. "Can't you do something?"

Her godmother shook her head no.

"I used to be able to . . . before . . .but now . . ." She held up her hands, helplessly. "I'm sorry. I'm so, so sorry."

Emerald collapsed in tears, feeling her heart breaking even more than it had when her friend was ordered to leave her. This couldn't be real, it just couldn't. She had come to save Eseland for Maple. Now Maple was gone.

The bang of the throne room doors flying open jolted everyone. All eyeballs turned to see the new arrival. A half-dozen knights came charging in on horseback, their swords drawn. They were flanked by four trolls, one of whom Emerald recognized as Mavis, the troll they'd met in the cave.

"King Spruce, lay down your arms. We have you surrounded!" the knight at the head of the pack exclaimed, his voice trailing off as he saw the scene before him.

"Daddy!" Emerald exclaimed in surprise as she stood up. Things were getting more surreal by the moment.

"Emerald?" Her father took his helmet off and looked closely at his daughter with concern. "Emerald, are you okay?" Then King Argos jumped off his horse and ran to his daughter, gathering her up in his arms as he reached her. "We got the wedding invitation from the king and came straight away," he said, pulling away and searching his daughter for any injury. "Your mother—she's a mess. We met up with the trolls in the woods on the way and they helped us get through Ortland."

"What about the giants?" Emerald asked, worried that Medina might still be under threat without the evil king to reverse his orders.

"Giants?" King Argos looked confused.

Relief swept through Emerald. King Spruce must have been bluffing about the giants. "Never mind." She smiled at her father. Better not to add any other worries to his plate right now.

"Your daughter is a hero, your Majesty," Emerald's godmother said, putting a hand on the king's arm. "A hero?" King Argos slowly looked around the room, his eyes widening in amazement and stopping on the motionless dragon's body.

"You did . . . all this?" "Well, er, yes," Emerald said, with almost as much bewilderment as the king.

"All hail Princess Emerald!" called out Filari suddenly. Slowly a chant began building throughout the room. "All hail Princess Emerald!"

Emerald stared around dizzily but managed to raise her hand and wave. The reality of what had happened with King Spruce and the dragon was slowly starting to sink in.

"Yes, yes, all hail the great Princess Emerald." The sound of a croaking voice rising above the chanting caused the crowd to fall silent. "Now where is my son?" Mavis stepped forward and looked accusingly at Emerald. The creatures standing nearest to the troll fell back in fright. Even the knights' horses pawed and snorted nervously.

Swallowing, Emerald took a step closer to Mavis and said, "I'm sorry, but we don't know where he is."

Mavis looked like she was about to hurt someone. Fortunately, a small voice perked up beside Emerald. "Actually, we do," said Raina. "He's in the dungeon. My father put him there when he, um, took over."

"And how do we know yer telling the truth?" Mavis asked suspiciously. "Yer the evil king's spawn, after all."

"I . . . it's the truth," Raina responded helplessly. She looked frightened.

"Is there someone who could go down and see if he's there?" Emerald asked, looking around the room. She had to do something to control the situation. A pair of muscular centaurs stepped forward.

"We'll go," one of them said.

"Thank you," Emerald replied. They bowed and left the room. Emerald turned and once again noticed Maple in Raina's arms. She felt the air go out of her as she collapsed next to the princess and imp.

"That yer friend?" Mavis asked, approaching the group. She still didn't sound friendly, but at least she seemed a bit less likely to snap.

"Yes," Emerald whispered. "She was crushed by the dragon."

"If Harry's here, he can probably help," Mavis said matter-of-factly. "He's good at that stuff."

Emerald looked up at her in hope and gratitude. Mavis simply sniffed and looked away.

"Emerald, it will be okay," Porter said softly to Emerald, putting his hand over hers.

"How are you doing?" Emerald looked up at him, realizing she hadn't checked on him yet.

"I have a few bruises and my head is still a little woozy, but I'll be okay. I just need to lay off the tallyweed in the future." He smiled at Emerald. She smiled back. She couldn't believe how many times she'd come close to losing Porter in the last few weeks. And yet here he was still at her side and supporting her once again. If it was anyone else, she was sure they would have run away by now. He was a true hero in her book. She resolved to protect him and their friendship with all her might from here on out.

After what seemed like an eternity, the two centaurs returned to the throne room holding up a very weak Harry. Though the chaos had died down, none of the creatures had left the room. They were milling around, looking worriedly at Emerald and her little group. The crowd made way for the centaurs, though, as the creatures gently escorted Harry to

Emerald. Clearly his time in the dungeon hadn't been easy. He looked weary and hungry, but otherwise uninjured.

"Oh, Harry!" both Elyria and Mavis said at the same time. He looked at them both and then back at the floor, ashamed.

"Yah clod!" Mavis said, but she gave her son a big hug.

"Maybe this time yah'll have learned yer lesson."

"Yes, Mother," he said dryly. "Good to see yah too."

"Harry," Elyria said more sternly. "Harry, you've created quite a mess with your stone."

"Yes, ma'am," Harry said, this time sounding properly abashed. "Ah'm sorry."

"Fortunately, this young lady saved the day." Elyria gestured grandly to Emerald. Harry's eyes went wide when he saw the young woman standing before him.

"Thank you, Miss, uh—"

"Princess Emerald," Elyria interrupted, giving Harry a stern look. "My goddaughter."

"Princess Emerald," he repeated in amazement, dropping to his knees.

"Rise, please, Harry." Emerald took his rough hands in hers and pulled him up. "Maybe you can save the day too. Your mother said you might be able to help my friend. She was crushed by the dragon."

Emerald stepped out of the way so Harry could see Maple. He stood but continued to make a couple of small bows as he walked past Emerald. He knelt when he reached Maple and put a hand on her forehead, touched her mouth, and then softly patted down the rest of her body. His forehead was furled in concentration.

"Yes, perhaps. It's bad, but just maybe," he muttered. "Her heart still beats. Very faint. But it beats."

"Please, oh please do something," Emerald pleaded.

"Ah, well, Ah might be able . . . Ah would need a unicorn,

though." Harry muttered to himself.

"Bia!" Emerald called as she stood and looked around for the unicorn, hoping she was still there.

"At your service," Bia's smooth voice came from the front of the room.

The crowds parted, leaving room for Bia to make her way to the little group. Even the creatures of Eseland, who were no strangers to unicorns, bowed reverently out of her way. Emerald could hear her father gasp and caught a ripple of excited, hushed chatter erupt from his knights. As many magical creatures as they'd seen since Medina started taking in refugees, there hadn't been a single unicorn. The pure majesty of a unicorn was enough to make any man or woman fall to his or her knees in gratitude for seeing such a wondrous sight.

"Oh, excellent. We might just have a chance," Harry said as Bia came to a stop next to him. "Ah need one of yer tears. She needs to drink it."

Bia nodded and bent over Maple's face as Harry gently opened the imp's mouth. A single silver tear fell from the unicorn's eye into Maple's mouth. Emerald watched in fascination.

"Unicorn tears have healing powers," explained Harry. He then put one hand on Maple's forehead and the other on his heart. Closing his eyes, Harry began to chant in a language Emerald didn't recognize. She saw beads of sweat form at his forehead as he chanted. It seemed like he went on for hours, but the entire room stayed silent and focused on Harry as he fought for Maple's life.

"Now what?" Emerald asked, when he finally finished, looking eagerly at Maple for any sign of life.

"Now, we wait," Harry said. "The unicorn's tear and my spell for life should give her a fighting chance. She needs to rest. But she shouldn't be moved far. Is there somewhere we can take her?"

"Please, you can have one of the rooms in our castle." The prince Raina was supposed to marry suddenly materialized next to Emerald's small gang. He bowed. "Guillaume Joseph Matthew Winchester the Third, at your service."

"Thank you, Prince Gee—" Emerald started, but the prince interrupted her.

"Just Guy is fine," he said, gallantly. "My family—my kingdom—and I are forever in your debt. If there's anything we can do."

"Just the room is fine for now," Emerald responded, smiling at him.

"Indeed," Prince Guy said. "Please, follow me."

Emerald nodded at her friends and Porter gently took Maple from Raina's arms. He followed the prince. Emerald and Filari helped Raina up and together they walked behind Porter. Emerald's godmother, Harry, and King Argos made up the rear of their little procession. The room was filled with a reverent silence as Emerald and her friends left. Emerald could feel all eyes on her. She was trying with all her might to keep her head up and not break down into worried sobs.

All they could do was wait.

Chapter Twenty-Two

GET BETTER MAPLE

It had been a full week since Emerald faced the dragon and Maple still had not opened her eyes. Emerald hadn't left her side. Prince Guy had given them the best room in the castle and Emerald slept on a tufted velvet chaise next to the carved wooden canopy bed in which Maple rested. Her friends, godmother, and father all came in from time to time and encouraged her to take a break for a meal or to at least step out for some air, but Emerald refused. She wouldn't leave her best friend.

"Maple, please don't leave me," Emerald murmured as she stroked the imp's pale face. "I can't live without you again."

A knock on the door startled her.

"Enter," she called, wiping her eyes on her sleeve. Her godmother had finally convinced her to change and she was now wearing a simple blue cotton gown borrowed from one of the castle maids.

Harry stepped into the room and closed the door. He walked over to the bed and looked thoughtfully down at Maple. He touched her head and felt at her wrist for a pulse. He then pushed the heavy down comforter back and gently moved her legs.

"She seems to be healing well, physically," Harry said, scrunching up his wrinkled face in concentration. "Perhaps the trauma was too much for her mind. Ah'll come back in a bit. Bring my blossom elixir and memory smoke again."

Harry had been working around the clock to try and heal Maple. He refused to give up. Emerald was forever grateful to him and felt he was more than making up for his mistakes with the stone.

"Would ya like a sleeping potion?" Harry asked, peering worriedly at Emerald's worn face. "Looks like ya could use a little rest."

"No. Thank you, Harry. I'll rest when . . ." Emerald's voice trailed off and she gestured toward Maple. Harry nodded understandingly and made his way back to the door. He turned before leaving as if to say something, but instead just smiled encouragingly at Emerald and stepped quietly out into the hall.

A few hours later, Emerald was awoken by another rap on the door. She jolted upright and wiped a small trail of saliva from her cheek. She couldn't believe she'd fallen asleep. She looked quickly at Maple but was relieved to see her friend was still breathing. She even seemed to have a little more color in her cheeks.

"Come in," Emerald called. The door opened and Raina walked in uncertainly. She hadn't been by since Maple was brought to the room. Emerald supposed she felt guilty for what her father had done and for Maple's injury.

"Hello, um, I just wanted to check on Maple," Raina said timidly as she approached the bed. "Is she getting better?"

"She seems to be, but she hasn't woken up yet."

"Oh." Raina fell silent for a bit, looking down at Maple. Emerald eventually noticed Raina was biting her bottom lip to keep from crying. Instantly she felt bad. Maple was still here, but Raina had lost her father. No matter how evil he was, losing him couldn't be easy for her.

"How are you?" Emerald asked Raina gently.

"Me? I, um, I'm . . . okay . . ." Raina choked before bursting into tears. "Sorry, I wasn't going to do this. Cry, I mean."

"It's okay," Emerald said, rising from the bed and walking around to Raina. She put her arms awkwardly around the young woman who had almost become her stepdaughter.

"I just wish I could go back," Raina sniffed, her sobs slowing a bit. "I wish I could stop him. Stop all of this before it started. He deserved it. But I do miss him. He was . . . he loved me."

"Your father?" Emerald asked, immediately regretting her obvious question.

"Yes, him." Raina looked up at Emerald with watery blue eyes. "And also, there's Prince Guy. He's been really sweet. I think I like him. But I'm afraid if his people see him with me they won't trust him."

Emerald nodded. "Perhaps take it slow. Do some small things to help the creatures of Eseland rebuild their lives. Take them food or help replant the area around the castle that was destroyed by vines. Let them see you aren't your father."

"Prince Guy says the same thing," Raina agreed, though her eyes still looked worried. "I know I can't go back. I just hope I can move forward."

"You can." Emerald smiled encouragingly. "And I'll help you too. I'll publicly declare and demonstrate our friendship."

"Oh, thank you, Emerald!" Raina threw her arms around the princess. "I know I don't deserve your kindness. I'm so sorry for the way I treated you."

"Well, we all do things we sometimes regret."

"Regret! Yes, I was supposed to tell you. Your mother is here to see you." Raina exclaimed. Emerald's eyes flew open in surprise. She'd been through a lot in the past couple of weeks, but she didn't know if she had the strength to see her mother yet.

"Should I send her in?" Raina asked, searching Emerald's face.

Emerald paused and then nodded. "Yes, of course. Please send her in."

After one more quick hug, Raina scuttled out of the room. Emerald waited with pounding heart for her mother to come in. She didn't want to leave Maple, but she also didn't know if her reunion with her mother was something that should play out in front of her injured friend. Before she could make a decision about staying or leaving, the door opened once again and her mother stepped in.

Emerald and her mother stared at each other uncertainly for a moment, but then a wave of relief crossed Queen Willow's face. She rushed over to Emerald and gathered her up in her arms. "Emerald, my daughter, I'm so happy to see you," she said, her voice thick with emotion. "When you ran off, I felt so guilty. I knew I'd pushed you too far. And when we got the invitation saying you were marrying King Spruce, I was so scared. I was so frightened that you were gone forever."

"I'm sorry, Mama. I really didn't mean to make you worry. I just couldn't face marrying Prince Eustace."

"I know, my darling," her mother responded. "I was so caught up in trying to make your life perfect that I didn't take the time to consider what you really needed—understanding. And acceptance. You are not me. You are not my mother. You are you and you are special."

"Thank you, Mama," Emerald said, hugging her mother again. "I shouldn't have run away. That wasn't very brave of me. I've learned it's not just enough to be physically strong. I also have to be strong in my beliefs."

"I think we've both learned a thing or two these past few weeks," Emerald's mother said, smiling.

"You did almost get your way, though," Emerald said.

"What do you mean?" her mother asked, cocking an eyebrow.

"Well, I almost married a king. And I would have had a

daughter right away," Emerald said, trying to keep a straight face.

Her mother's face went pale. "He was definitely not who I had in mind for your husband," Queen Willow said weakly.

"Well, the wedding fell through. He didn't even make it to the feast. I guess you could say he became the feast," Emerald said, bursting out laughing. Queen Willow joined in. The two of them couldn't stop laughing, but it was more from relief than hilarity.

"If that's your idea of a wedding, Emerald, please don't invite me to the next one," a small voice, punctuated by the sound of munching, squeaked behind Emerald.

"Maple!"

Chapter Twenty-Three

HAPPILY EVER AFTER . . . UNTIL THE NEXT ADVENTURE

A crowd gathered to see Emerald and her family off on their return journey home. The air was filled with music and laughter. As the dust settled from the traumatic rise and fall of King Spruce, the creatures of Eseland moved from shock into celebration. A few days after Maple awoke, Prince Guy and his family, who were restored from being frozen in stone, hosted a ball to honor Emerald for saving the kingdom. Nearly a week later, the festive atmosphere still filled the land.

"It is with great sadness that we bid farewell to the great Princess Emerald and her friends and family," proclaimed Prince Guy to the gathered crowds at the moment of Emerald and her entourage's departure. "But we have made a bond for life. If ever Medina should need our help, we will be there. And I believe Medina will do the same for us."

Emerald smiled and nodded. Her parents nodded as well. Prince Guy bowed deeply and a cheer went up from the crowd. Raina ran over to Emerald and flung her arms around her new friend.

"I'll hope you'll include me in that bond for life," Raina whispered in Emerald's ear. Emerald hugged her tightly and whispered back, "I will." The girls grinned at each other after they pulled away. Raina bounded back to stand near Prince Guy. It seemed things were going well between the two of them.

"May I help you onto your horse?" Porter stepped next to Emerald and held out a hand to her. He had fully recovered in the days after the wedding fiasco. They both flushed a bit as their eyes met. King Argos and Queen Willow both noticed the look that passed between them and exchanged their own, interested look. Perhaps something more than just a friendship was brewing here.

"Thank you," Emerald said softly as Porter boosted her up onto her horse. She was glad that not only had her parents welcomed Porter back to the castle with open arms, they had also asked him to more formally continue Emerald's archery, sword fighting, and horseback lessons. It looked like the two of them would be spending a lot more time together. Emerald smiled happily to herself.

"You know, I just realized that Porter is very handsome," Maple whispered slyly to Emerald after Porter boosted her up behind the princess.

"Oh hush." Emerald flushed, gripping the reins and trying to fight the instinct to steal another glance at Porter.

"I'm just saying," Maple responded innocently as she wrapped her arms around Emerald's waist. "I think he thinks you are quite pretty too."

"Maple!" Emerald exclaimed. Her face and neck were now as red as her hair. Maple laughed. Emerald couldn't be too upset at the little imp. It was good to hear her laughing again.

A trumpet sounded and Emerald and her party were off. Emerald touched the cord around her neck attached to the pouch holding her guiding stone. It had been recovered from the evil king's cottage. She was grateful to have it back. She wouldn't need it on this journey, but it gave her a sense of comfort. She needed that right now. Emerald was a little nervous about her return to Medina. So much had changed since she left. Not only was she filled with a new confidence and inner strength, her parents had also agreed to postpone her search for a fiancé. She was going to be allowed to do things her way. Of course, some people (namely her grandmother) weren't going to be happy, but her parents now recognized that Emerald had to form her own path to become the queen she was meant to be.

Emerald could hear Maple humming happily behind her. Whatever happened next, Emerald knew she was surrounded by friends and family who loved and supported her.

To Emerald's happy surprise, she was welcomed back in Medina with almost as much fanfare as she'd received before she left Eseland. Highly exaggerated stories were already flying around about Emerald's adventure and she was greeted by stares of awe and admiration whenever she went out.

"I heard you battled two dragons," Maple said with a giggle as she watched Porter critique Emerald's grip on her bow and arrow one afternoon a few days after their return.

"And I heard King Spruce cast a love spell on you, but you were too strong and broke his heart instead." Porter grinned at her.

"Oh, shush, you two. I'm just glad the whole thing is over."

"Me too," Porter agreed.

"Me three," Maple piped up, not wanting to be left out. She popped a bit of muffin in her mouth. "You know, there aren't much better bakers in the world than those in Medina. I think we should stick around here for a while."

Emerald smiled fondly at her friend. She was happy to be home. Her adventure had stretched her emotionally and physically, making her equally more grateful for her life in Medina as well as more confident in the person she was becoming. It was fun to reminisce about the things she and her friends had seen and done, but it would be a lie to say she wasn't glad it was over.

"Princess Emerald, Princess Emerald!" The baker's son broke her reverie with his frantic cries as he darted over the lawn to where Emerald was practicing her archery. Throckton, too, had grown up since his days of tormenting the refugee children from Eseland. He was especially more respectful of Emerald and her friends since learning about them defeating the evil king and slaying a dragon.

"Come quick," he huffed and puffed as he reached the princess, bending over to catch his breath. "There's trouble brewing to the south. Your father and mother sent for you to come as fast as possible. They need your help."

Emerald looked at her friends and grinned.

So much for sticking around Medina for a while.

ACKNOWLEDGEMENTS

It may seem odd to thank myself, but I would be wrong in not acknowledging the awkward twelve-year-old girl who wrote and illustrated the original Emerald story for an art class project. I am grateful that my seventh-grade self so loved fairytales and writing that she created the inspiration for my first published book. Like Emerald, she marched to the beat of her own drum.

I would also like to acknowledge my husband, Matt, for his unending support and belief in me. His feedback over multiple drafts of the book was as thoughtful and valuable as if he was a professional editor. Thank you, Matt, for investing so much time and energy in helping me make my writing dreams come true.

My gratitude also extends to my mom for her support and early edits, as well as to my editor for helping guide the completion of my first book. A special thanks to my designer who brought my characters to life through her great illustrations—they were a massive improvement over my seventh-grade scribbles.

Finally, thank you to all you readers for joining me on this magical adventure. I hope you enjoy Emerald and her world as much as I do.

ABOUT THE AUTHOR

Becky Biggs is a loyal subject to the pen and an adventurous princess at heart. She has been imagining new worlds and fun characters since she could first write. Her Emerald series was inspired by a story she wrote and illustrated for a seventh-grade art class. That book lay buried in a trunk for twenty-some years before it magically captured her imagination again. She recently unleashed the enchanted characters and worlds of Eseland and Medina with the first book in her series, *Emerald and the Elf King*.

When she's not writing, Becky enjoys setting off on international adventures. Her worlds are inspired by her travels around the globe, particularly through the time she spent living in France and Germany. She is married to her own Prince Charming and is the mother of two royally darling children.

If you want to continue to follow Emerald's adventures, visit www.beckybiggs.com and sign up for the mailing list.

CPSIA information can be obtained
at www.ICGtesting.com
Printed in the USA
FFHW02n0719130818
47730666-51394FF